What a babe . . .

I shook my head, trying to shift my focus back to Elizabeth's surfing skills. This was getting a little crazy. For one thing, I was supposed to be teaching her the ways of the wave. For another, I'd liked Elizabeth since the day I met her—but crushing on her hadn't gotten me anywhere up until this point, and I didn't think it was going to get me anywhere now. Besides, I was pretty sure I wasn't her type.

Taking a deep breath, I placed my hands on her waist to help her find the right stance on the board. As soon as I gave her a gentle push, though, she started totally cracking up.

I yanked my hands away. "What's wrong, dude?" I asked in alarm.

"Sorry, Blue," Elizabeth said breathlessly after a moment, when she finally had her laughter under control. "I'm really sorry about that. I guess I just—well, I'll show you."

Before I could react, she turned and started tickling me. "Whoa!" I shouted. I was so startled that I stepped backward and tripped over my own feet, sprawling flat on my back in the sand. Giggling wildly, Elizabeth came after me.

Don't miss any of the books in SWEET VALLEY JUNIOR HIGH, an exciting series from Bantam Books!

Clueless

Written by
Jamie Suzanne

Created by
FRANCINE PASCAL

BANTAM BOOKS
NEW YORK · TORONTO · LONDON · SYDNEY · AUCKLAND

RL 4, 008-012

CLUELESS

A Bantam Book / December 2000

Sweet Valley Junior High is a trademark of Francine Pascal.
Conceived by Francine Pascal.
Cover photography by Michael Segal.

Produced by 17th Street Productions,
an Alloy Online, Inc. company.
33 West 17th Street
New York, NY 10011.

ISBN: 0-553-48726-4

Visit us on the Web! www.randomhouse.com/kids

Published simultaneously in the United States and Canada

Bantam Books is an imprint of Random House Children's Books, a
division of Random House, Inc. BANTAM BOOKS and the rooster
colophon are registered trademarks of Random House, Inc. Bantam Books,
1540 Broadway, New York, New York 10036.

PRINTED IN THE UNITED STATES OF AMERICA

OPM   0 9 8 7 6 5 4 3 2 1

To Richard Wenk

Elizabeth

Think, Wakefield, I told myself. Think,
think, think!

It was no use. I still didn't have a single decent suggestion for the next issue of *Zone*, the online magazine I'd started with my friends. That was a bit of a problem since I was sitting in a meeting, discussing that exact topic: new story ideas. Salvador del Valle was blabbing on and on about *his* idea to write the whole next issue in pig latin.

"What do you think, Elizabeth?" Anna Wang said, glancing at me and tucking a strand of black hair behind one ear. I think she was just trying to get Salvador to shut up. We'd already told him a million times that the pig-latin thing would never work. But once Salvador gets something in his head, it's hard to get it out of there.

Brian Rainey and Blue Spiccoli turned to look at me too. Even Salvador shrugged and leaned back in his chair. I guess they were all waiting for me to come up with something brilliant.

Elizabeth

I gulped, scanning my brain for some sudden inspiration. But it stayed a big blank, just like it had been for the past few days. What was wrong with me? I usually had tons of ideas for stories. I'd always loved writing—it sometimes seemed like I'd never have enough time to write down all the stories bouncing around inside my head. So where had all those ideas gone?

My friends were still staring at me. I cleared my throat, then pretended to cough, stalling for time. "Um," I said at last. "Uh."

"Spit it out," Salvador said, leaning over and patting me on the back.

What was I supposed to say? I couldn't admit that I didn't have a single decent idea. Glancing down at the scribbles on my notepad, I grimaced. Somehow I didn't think an article called "New Paint in the Cafeteria: Pro or Con?" was going to impress anyone. One about the janitor's new vacuum cleaner probably wouldn't go over too well either. I glanced up and noticed Blue watching me. I swallowed hard. Blue had recently joined *Zone*. What if he thought I *never* had any good ideas?

I glanced around the room desperately. We were meeting in Ms. Upton's classroom. Seeing a clutter of papers tacked near the door, I blurted out the first thing that popped into my head.

"How about an article called 'Top-Ten Tips for a Neater Bulletin Board'?"

I winced as soon as the idiotic words left my mouth. Salvador let out a bark of laughter. "Good one, Elizabeth!" he cried, tossing back his head of curly, dark brown hair. "We could do a follow-up piece called 'Fifty Ways to Reuse Chalk Dust.' The teachers would love it!"

"No way," Brian Rainey put in with a grin. "If we want to appeal to the teachers, we should start printing a gossip column. Have you ever heard them blabbing to one another in the teachers' lounge? It sounds like a soap opera in there sometimes. No joke."

I laughed along with the others, relieved that everyone thought I was kidding with that lame story idea. "In that case, how about an article called 'The Secret Lives of the Lunch Ladies'?" I suggested, stalling for more time.

"Dude," Blue said. "That would totally rule. But you know, it might be too tame for our teachers. How about one called 'SVJH Teacher Gives Birth to Alien Baby'?"

I laughed again with everyone else. Blue's eyes were sparkling, making him look really cute. Not that he's not always pretty cute. He's got this sun-bleached blond hair and a great smile. When he first joined *Zone*, I was a little surprised. I'd figured that story meetings and research and deadlines weren't his kind of thing at all. But I've learned since then that even though Blue acts like this totally laid-back, clueless surfer dude, he's really smart and interesting.

"Good one, Blue," Anna said, smiling. "But seriously, now. Elizabeth, do you—"

"I've got a good idea for a follow-up article," I interrupted. I could tell Anna was about to try to bring the meeting back to order, and I didn't want to let it happen. She had to leave soon to meet some friends from drama club, and Salvador had a doctor's appointment. All I had to do was stall until then—or until I actually came up with a real story idea. Whichever came first. "How about 'Alien Baby Abducts SVJH Student'?"

"Excellent!" Salvador exclaimed. "But we shouldn't focus just on aliens. We really ought to give werewolves and swamp monsters some coverage too if we want to be taken seriously as journalists."

We tossed around a few more silly ideas before Anna glanced at the clock on the wall over the door. "Hey, I've got to go," she said.

Whew. I gathered up my stuff and tossed it into my backpack. *What a relief,* I thought. *It seemed like that stupid meeting was never going to end.*

I immediately felt bad for thinking that. Usually *Zone* meetings are just about my favorite part of the week. Of course, usually I have something to contribute other than goofy jokes. I hurried out of the classroom behind Anna, my brain feeling completely numb.

I'd never really been sure what people meant when they said they had writer's block.

Now I understood.

Jessica

"Later, guys," I sang out, slinging my gym bag over my shoulder and heading for the locker-room door. "I'd better go. If I miss the late bus again and have to call home for a ride, my brother will kill me."

"See you, Jessica," Bethel McCoy said, lifting her fingers from her shoelaces just long enough to wave. The rest of my teammates chimed in with their good-byes.

I waved and left, wishing for about the millionth time that I didn't always have to rush off after track practice. That's the trouble with living halfway across town from school. Ever since my twin sister, Elizabeth, and I got rezoned to Sweet Valley Junior High, we have to schedule our whole lives around the stupid bus.

As I stepped out onto the sidewalk, blinking in the late afternoon California sunshine, I spotted a girl with blondish-brownish curls flying all over the place like a big cloud. Kristin Seltzer has amazing hair. I like my long, blond hair and all, but sometimes it's a little boring.

"Hey!" I called out. "Kristin!"

Kristin turned and waited for me to catch up. "Hi, Jessica," she said. When she smiles, she gets these totally adorable dimples in her cheeks. "Did you just get out of track practice?"

"Yeah." I fell into step beside her, glancing ahead to make sure the late bus wasn't there yet. "What about you? I didn't know there was a student-government meeting today."

"There wasn't. I had to stay after to meet with Mrs. Bertram." Kristin rolled her eyes. She's really smart—usually her grades are just as perfect as my twin's—but she's been having a little trouble in English lately. Personally, I think she's just way too distracted by all the stuff she does as president of the eighth grade. Which is understandable. I'm sure that planning school dances and carnivals and stuff is way more interesting than English class.

"Oh," I said sympathetically. "Bummer. I thought maybe you were planning for the school Olympics." Kristin had been planning for the Olympics for a couple of weeks now. According to a plan she and Bethel had put together with the rest of the student council, the whole school was going to be divided into teams, like the different countries that compete in the real Olympics. The committee had come up with a bunch of different events that would take place over five days—a swim meet, a few different team sports, and of course some track events. I was definitely psyched for that last part. Next to Bethel, I'm the fastest runner on the track team.

Kristin shrugged. "I don't have to do anything for that right now," she said. "Most of the planning's done. We just have to wait for Mr. Todd to feed the names of all the students into the office computer to decide the teams."

"Cool." I checked my watch. There were still a couple of hours until dinnertime. "Do you want to come over for a while?" A few months ago, when Kristin and I first met, I would have felt a little nervous about inviting her to hang at my house. I mean, she is one of the most popular, well-liked people in school, and I haven't exactly had the easiest time fitting in at Sweet Valley Junior High. Plus I have to admit that at first, I really wanted to get on Kristin's good side because she was so popular. But that was right after my twin, Elizabeth, and I had been rezoned from Sweet Valley Middle School, where being popular was the most important thing in the world to me. But now I'm Kristin's friend because she's one of the nicest people I've ever met, and I always feel comfortable around her.

I grinned to myself. It's funny how things usually work out for the better, even when they don't work out the way you think they should. I glanced over at Kristin, but she looked worried. "I'd love to come over, but I can't," she said, glancing at her watch. "I'm supposed to meet—"

"There you are, Kristin. I've been waiting for*ever*."

I winced at the familiar voice. Kristin turned and smiled at the dark-haired girl lounging against the brick wall of the school. "Hey, Lacey," she said. "Sorry I'm late. Mrs. Bertram kept blabbing on and on about the real meaning behind the classic Greek epics."

"Whatever. It's okay." Lacey Frells glanced at me coolly. She was wearing one of her highly fashionable outfits—skintight black jeans, a slinky red shirt, and her favorite black combat boots. "Aren't you late for your school bus, Jessica?"

Somehow she made it sound like riding the bus was about the dorkiest idea in the history of the universe. Not that I disagree. But she didn't have to be so snotty about it. Of course, her attitude wasn't surprising. Lacey Frells was the biggest reason I'd had such a hard time fitting in at Sweet Valley Junior High during the first few months I came here. I'd tried really hard to be her friend at first, and time after time she'd used me, lied to me, and made me feel like a complete idiot. These days I try to be civil to her because she's Kristin's best friend, and sometimes I even manage to have conversations with her that aren't completely rude, but I still have no idea what Kristin sees in her.

"Yeah," I said tightly. "I've got to catch the bus. I don't have a high-school boyfriend to drive me around." Then I put my hand over my mouth, pretending to be apologetic. "Oops! Of course, neither do you."

Well, I said I *try* to be civil. Lacey scowled at me. She'd recently broken up with her loser boyfriend, Gel. "Maybe not," she snapped, "but at least I have a *life*."

"Guys," Kristin put in, sounding kind of desperate.

I bit my tongue, trying to be good for Kristin's sake. Glancing down the sidewalk, I spotted the bus pulling in. That was my cue to get out of Lacey's face before things went any further. As much as Lacey irritates me, I've realized she's not really worth fighting with, especially if I want to stay friends with Kristin. So it's better all around if Lacey and I just stay out of each other's way as much as possible.

"Catch you later, Kristin," I said, ignoring Lacey.

Kristin said good-bye, then hustled Lacey off down the sidewalk. I turned in the opposite direction, not bothering to hurry. The late-activities bus always sits around forever, waiting for kids to get out of their practices and meetings and rehearsals.

I had almost reached the bus when I spotted my twin coming out of the doors at the far end of the building. But who was the blond guy she was walking with? I squinted. The sun was in my eyes, but I could tell that it definitely wasn't her goofy friend Salvador. Or Brian Rainey either.

Oh, I realized when they got a little closer. *It's just her new best buddy, Blue.*

For some reason, Elizabeth had been spending all kinds of time with Blue Spiccoli lately. Which was totally baffling to me since, besides being on the same volleyball team, they have absolutely nothing in common. Blue is so laid-back, he's practically comatose. He spends way more time surfing and hanging at the beach than he does at school. Not that I can blame him for that. If I lived on the beach with my older brother and no parents, I'd probably ditch school and have fun all the time too. But not Elizabeth. She's the opposite of mellow, especially when it comes to school.

So what could she and Blue possibly have to talk about? Whatever it was, it looked like they were both totally into it. They were only about a hundred yards away now, and Elizabeth still hadn't noticed me standing there by the bus, staring at them.

Hmmm, I thought, suddenly forgetting all about Lacey and how easy it was for her to push my buttons. *Could good old straight-A, floss-every-night Liz actually have a crush on Blue?* I watched more carefully as Elizabeth and Blue continued wandering slowly toward the bus, still totally wrapped up in their conversation. *Weirder things have happened, right? Not many, but you never know.*

Elizabeth

"So I thought Sal had some radical story ideas," Blue said, shifting his book bag from one shoulder to the other. He'd caught up with me after the *Zone* meeting broke up, and now he was walking with me toward my bus, which was already idling at the curb. "He's really funny, you know?"

I tried not to stare at the way his muscles sort of rippled when he moved his bag. Blue lives right on the beach and surfs all the time, which is probably why he's in such good shape. "Um, what?" I said, realizing I had no idea what he had just said.

"I said that Sal's one funny dude." Blue laughed. "That pig-latin thing is hilarious. And Anna—she's always got about a million new ideas for cool stories. Brian too. How do you guys do it?"

"Don't ask me," I muttered, flashing back to that horrible moment during the meeting when I'd realized I had absolutely nothing to say.

13

Blue shot me a surprised look. "What's up, Elizabeth?" he said. "You sound a little weird. Is everything cool?"

I sighed, wishing I'd just kept quiet. The last thing I wanted to do was admit that I'd suddenly turned into a total failure as a writer. "I'm okay."

"Really?" Blue turned to peer into my face. "You don't look okay."

His blue eyes looked so concerned that I was tempted to just blurt out the whole thing. I was surprised by that feeling. This wasn't the kind of thing I would admit to most people—not Anna and Salvador, or my parents, or maybe even Jessica. But for some reason I felt like I could trust Blue. Maybe because I hadn't really known him that long, so I didn't have that much to lose. Or because he had such a total live-and-let-live attitude—I figured he wouldn't judge me.

I took a deep breath. "Okay, here's the problem. I haven't written one word for the next issue of *Zone*," I admitted. "I haven't even come up with a single decent idea. My mind is a total blank." I bit my lip and glanced at him. "I think I may have writer's block. And I don't know what to do about it."

"Whoa. That's harsh." Blue shook his head, looking sympathetic. "But you really shouldn't let it get you down. I bet even the greatest writers *ever* get blocked sometimes. It's all just part of the process, you know?"

"Really?" That actually made me feel a little better.

"Definitely," Blue said. "I bet it's kind of like when the waves are way choppy and you can't catch a decent one to save your life. After a while, it's usually better to start fresh—like, try a different beach, or a different board, or whatever. Get a new outlook."

I smiled despite my worries. "Do you compare *everything* to surfing?" I teased.

"Sure," he replied with a grin. "Surfing's the meaning of life, you know." He stopped short. "Yo! I've got it! Why don't you do an article on surfing?"

"What?" I raised one eyebrow. "You're kidding, right? What I know about surfing would fill about one sentence."

"No, listen." Blue sounded excited. "I could teach you how to surf. Then you could write about it."

I blinked at him in surprise. He wanted to teach me to surf? A couple of weeks ago he'd given Brian surfing lessons, and I'd been a little jealous. It had sounded like a lot of fun at the time. But to be honest, the thought made me a little nervous now. Blue's an awesome surfer.

15

Elizabeth

And me? Well, let's just say that Jessica's the athlete in our family. Just going out for the intramural volleyball team was a huge leap for me.

Still, I had to admit that an article about surfing could attract a whole new audience for *Zone*—there were lots of surfer dudes and beach bunnies around who would probably love it. Not to mention that it would mean spending a whole lot more time with Blue. He's an awesome friend.

"You know," I said thoughtfully, smiling at Blue, "that's a fantastic idea!"

Blue

I grinned at Elizabeth, psyched that she liked my idea. Her pretty blue-green eyes sort of danced when she smiled at me. I knew she would love surfing once she got the hang of it. Then we could spend tons of time hanging out at the beach together, soaking up rays between runs—

"There's just one problem," Elizabeth said, interrupting my daydream.

"What?" I was afraid she was going to say the problem was me—she didn't think I could teach her. I guess I don't really give off that teacherly kind of vibe. Actually, I haven't always been the most responsible guy in the world when it comes to being a student, let alone a teacher. But lately I'd been trying to get my act together at school. Elizabeth had been helping, even if she didn't know it. She'd been, like, totally inspirational when it came to being cool with school.

She shrugged, then stopped walking to turn and face me. She looked kind of worried. "I

17

know you did a great job teaching Brian," she said. "But you know sports aren't really my thing. I doubt I'll be as good at it as he was."

"No big," I said. "Even if you don't become a pro, it'll be a radical new thing for you, right? And that will give you a fresh outlook on your writing too. Get it?"

She looked thoughtful. "Yeah," she said. "I guess I do. It's just—" She took a deep breath and smiled weakly. "It looks pretty hard."

"No way," I assured her. "You just have to get in the zone, and then it's all good." I laughed. "Get it? In the *Zone*!"

"Okay," she said slowly, barely smiling at my joke. Admittedly it was pretty lame. "But I just don't know if a total newbie like me will have that much to say about it after just a few lessons."

I could already feel my beautiful beach daydream slipping away. Luckily inspiration struck again. It must have been a really good karma day for me. "Maybe it could be like a point-counterpoint kind of thing," I suggested. "You know the surfing competition Brian and I were in? Well, they're doing the girl's competition next week. You could enter that one, then we could both write about the two contests and what it took to get ready for them."

"Whoa. Wait a second. A *competition?*" Elizabeth sounded dubious.

"Don't worry—it's not like anyone will expect you to win or anything," I said. "But I'm sure you'll do okay, you know?" I added quickly. I'd almost forgotten—Elizabeth isn't like me. She actually cares about stuff like winning, at least sometimes. Well, I guess it's not really winning as much as it is about doing the best she can possibly do. She's kind of a perfectionist that way. "Besides," I added, inspiration hitting again, "you were so gung ho about encouraging Brian to go for it. I'm pretty surprised that you wouldn't take your own advice."

Elizabeth looked thoughtful again. "Well . . . How many people have you taught to surf, besides Brian?"

I grinned weakly, kicking at the sidewalk with the toe of my sandal. "One, besides him," I said. "After I teach you, that is."

She laughed. Then she took a deep breath and let it out slowly. "Well, okay," she said finally. "But still—are you sure it's possible to go from an absolute beginner to competition worthy in a week?"

"Way sure," I told her confidently. "Brian did it."

Elizabeth cocked an eyebrow. "Brian didn't make it up onto the *board*. If I'm going to be in the competition, I want to at least ride a wave or two."

I laughed. It's not really like Elizabeth to be so blunt. But then, she's pretty intense about anything she puts her mind to. And she had a point—Brian had been munched by the waves a couple of times during his first competition. "He still had a great time," I offered. "Besides, I'd hardly given him any lessons before the competition. I'll give *you* all the private training you can handle for the next week. And if you're still worried, I'll throw in a bonus."

"What?" Elizabeth asked.

"You can have unlimited use of my lucky surfboard," I told her. "It's never been touched by human hands. Other than mine, I mean."

Elizabeth looked surprised, a faint smile playing on her lips. "Really? And you'll let me use it?"

"Sure." I was majorly surprised myself since I didn't even know I was going to make the offer until it popped out. It wasn't the kind of thing I'd do for just anybody. I'm pretty easygoing about most stuff, but my lucky surfboard is different. Even my older brother, Leaf, and my friend Rick knew better than to mess with it.

What is it about Elizabeth Wakefield anyway? I wondered. She totally has this weird effect on me.

Then she shot me one of her killer smiles, and I remembered what it was about her. She was basically the cutest and coolest girl I'd ever met, and I wanted to hang out with her as much as possible. Even if that meant sharing my lucky surfboard. She totally deserved the honor.

"Thanks, Blue," she said shyly, making me think maybe she understood how big a deal this lucky-surfboard thing was. That just made me like her even more. "That would be great."

"Cool." I grinned at her. Suddenly the next week was looking to be majorly cool. "So when should we start?"

She glanced at the late bus, which had just belched a huge splurt of stinky exhaust as its motor chugged into life. "How about tomorrow after school?"

"Sounds like a plan," I agreed. I waved as she hurried toward the bus, then turned toward home.

Yep, I thought. *The next week is definitely going to be awesome!*

Instant Messages

KGrl99: Jessica?

WakefieldSV: Hi, Kristin!

KGrl99: Whassup?

WakefieldSV: Not much. Homework. Algebra stinx.

KGrl99: I hear you. Big news—I saw the final list of teams for the school Olympics.

WakefieldSV: Really? R we on the same team?

KGrl99: Well, I'm not on any team because I'm a judge. But you and Damon are on the same team.

WakefieldSV: Yesss! Who else?

KGrl99: You're not gonna be 2 happy.

WakefieldSV: Tell me!

KGrl99: Lacey.

WakefieldSV: What????????????????????????? No way. U have 2 do something!

KGrl99: What can I do? The computer picks the teams. Can't you guys just try to get along for a week?

WakefieldSV: No offense, but I just don't think I can handle it!

KGrl99: Chill, Jess! It's not that big a deal.

WakefieldSV: U R kidding, right?

KGrl99: I can't do anything. Not unless you want me to hack into the school computer system or something.

WakefieldSV: Hey, if that's what it takes . . .

KGrl99: Ha-ha. BTW, don't spread this around. The teams aren't supposed to be announced till next week.

WakefieldSV: Don't worry. Not like I want to brag about this.

Anna

"... so then Blue offered to write a sort of companion article to go along with mine," Elizabeth said. "You know, giving the boy's perspective."

Switching the phone to my other ear, I tried to focus on what she was talking about. I was feeling a little distracted. "Uh-huh," I said. "That reminds me. Did I tell you about the exercise we did in drama club today? Mr. Dowd had all the girls act like boys and vice versa. Toby pretended to be this grumpy old lady who talks to her cats."

I couldn't help smiling when I thought about Toby. He's this great guy I met when I joined drama club, and it's hard to believe I didn't know him before that. I mean, we aren't exactly boyfriend-girlfriend yet, but recently we admitted that we like each other. We've held hands a few times—that's about it.

"Hmmm. Anyway, like I was saying," Elizabeth continued, "Blue's going to give me lessons for the next week. And he wants me to enter this surfing contest weekend after next."

"Wow," I said, doing my best to tune in to what she was saying. After all, Elizabeth is one of my best friends. The least I could do was pay attention instead of thinking about Toby.

"Anyway, it should be interesting," Elizabeth went on. "Blue is even letting me use his lucky surfboard."

This time I couldn't help noticing that Elizabeth sounded a little weird. Not in a bad way—just different. Her voice was sort of breathless, like she was jogging on a treadmill while she talked. Ever since I joined the school's drama club, I've started noticing funny little details like that more. That sort of thing can really give you clues to people's moods and personalities and stuff.

So what's up with Elizabeth? I wondered. She sort of reminded me of someone—that odd breathless voice, I mean. But who?

"Hey," I blurted out as the answer finally dawned on me. Elizabeth reminded me of *myself!* I'd caught myself sounding that way a lot lately—mostly when I was talking about Toby. And Elizabeth had been spending an awful lot of time with Blue lately . . . "Wait a minute," I went on. "So these lessons with Blue—are these sort of, like, you know, dates?"

"No!" she responded before I could even finish the sentence, sounding slightly annoyed. "Of course not. I told you—we're working on a story together. As friends. Nothing more. No big deal."

"Really? Because you can tell me if you like him, you know. I think he's really cu—"

"Really," she said firmly, cutting me off. "Blue and I are friends. What's so strange about friends doing something like this? You and Salvador work together on stories all the time. So do Brian and I. It doesn't mean anything."

"Oh. Okay, whatever." I wasn't totally convinced. For some reason, I started thinking about this line from a scene Mr. Dowd had us read once in drama club—*The lady doth protest too much, methinks.* It's from Shakespeare. Methinks it is anyway.

And methinks maybe something is going on between Elizabeth and Blue, I thought with a secret smile. *Even if she won't admit it.*

Jessica

I sat at the desk in my bedroom, tapping my pencil on my algebra book. But I couldn't focus on the boring problem sets I was supposed to be doing. Ever since I'd gotten that IM from Kristin half an hour earlier, I couldn't think about anything else. Not that it's too hard to distract me from algebra any day of the week. But this was major.

I can't believe I'm getting stuck with Lacey for Olympics week, I thought grimly. *That stupid school computer must have it in for me. Either that or I have the worst luck in the entire universe.*

I sighed, imagining how horrible it was going to be having Lacey in my face all week. I mean, it was one thing to have to see her in the halls and in some of my classes. But to have her on my *team?* I've been running track long enough to know how important it is to have teammates you can trust if you want to have any chance of winning or even if you just want to be able to have fun. And I'd been looking

29

forward to having the chance to do both of those things during Olympics week. But now I knew I was just going to be miserable.

Like I said, Lacey gets her jollies from tormenting me. I know she calls me Jessica Lamefield behind my back. And it's not like she'd ever stop there. *Before I know it, she'll probably turn my whole team against me,* I thought, leaning my elbow on my textbook. *Talk about killer competition. Who knew the biggest test at the school Olympics would be surviving my own team?*

I grimaced at the thought. Talk about sheer torture. A week with Lacey was going to be downright brutal. *If she even bothers to show up for the events, that is.*

I brightened at that thought. Maybe she would just ditch the entire thing. That sounded like something she would do.

Then I remembered that Mr. Todd, our principal, had already announced that he'd be taking attendance throughout the events, and anyone who tried to ditch would get double detention. So chances were, Lacey would be there. Major bummer.

Why couldn't the stupid school computer have stuck some other team with Lacey? I thought irritably, glaring at my algebra book. It really didn't seem fair. At least my boyfriend, Damon, was going to be on my team, along with some other friends. But still. Basically I would rather be stuck with a team full of dorks like my locker partner, Ronald Rheece, than have to deal with *one* Lacey Frells.

Ronald Rheece. I turned and stared at the computer on my desk, thinking of something Kristin had said in her instant message. *Wait a minute.*

It was so obvious. My computer-genius locker partner was the perfect person to help me out of this mess! Ronald is a charter member of the computer club, along with the math club and the science club and every other boring club at school. If anyone could hack into the school's files and change the teams around, he could.

There was just one serious flaw in my plan. Asking Ronald for help would mean I'd have to talk to him. And that's something I generally try to avoid. He may be a genius, but he's totally clueless when it comes to the important things in life, like carrying on a conversation about something other than calculus.

Still, the more I thought about it, the more it seemed like the perfect solution. I definitely had to take action. Otherwise Lacey and I would probably end up killing each other. And Kristin would end up right smack in the middle.

31

I didn't want to do that to her. No way.

There's no way poor Kristin could deal with that, I told myself. *No way she could possibly juggle her two best friends fighting like cats and dogs and still have fun and set a good example for the rest of the school at the same time. She already has enough to handle as one of the judges.*

When I thought about it that way, getting Ronald to change Lacey to another team was practically an act of charity. Or at least an act of school spirit.

Jumping up from my desk, I headed for my bedroom door. If I was going to beg for Ronald's help, I might as well get it over with. I certainly didn't want to do it at school, with witnesses and everything. I rifled through my top desk drawer and pulled out my school directory.

Out in the hall I was just in time to see Elizabeth hanging up the phone. "Are you done with that?" I asked, reaching for the receiver. "I have to make a call."

"Huh?" Elizabeth blinked at me. "Oh. Yeah. Whatever. I was just talking to Anna."

She looked kind of annoyed, and she frowned a little when she said Anna's name. *Interesting,* I thought. *I wonder what that's all about?*

But if something was really bugging Elizabeth, I'd make sure to find out later. Dragging the phone into my room, I closed the door. I didn't want anyone to overhear me.

"Good evening, Rheece residence," a polite voice answered when I called Ronald's number. "This is Ronald. How can I help you?"

I rolled my eyes. Somehow Ronald's dorkiness came shining through even over the phone. "Hi, Ronald," I said. "This is Jessica."

"Jessica?" Ronald replied uncertainly. "Jessica who?"

"Jessica *Wakefield*." I rolled my eyes.

"Oh! Hi, Jessica," he said. "It's funny you should call. Well, not funny, exactly—more like ironic. You see, I was just thinking about you during biology class today."

"You were?" That was a little frightening. I wasn't sure I wanted to hear why.

"Uh-huh," Ronald went on. "See, we were discussing the fight-or-flight instinct in tigers who battle for territory. The description reminded me of the way you behave in the lunchroom sometimes."

I sighed. "Whatever. Look, Ronald, I have a very important question for you. Just how good are you at computer-type stuff?"

"My computer skills are excellent," Ronald replied. He launched into some long-winded explanation, going into all kinds of boring detail about stuff like gigabytes and DOS and RAM. "Why do you ask?" he finished at last.

I had to think about that one for a second. Ronald's response had made me a little dizzy. "Here's the thing," I said. "I have a little problem." I quickly filled him in on the basics—namely, that a cruel twist of fate had stuck me with Lacey, and I wanted to get myself unstuck. "So I figure the best way to fix the problem is to go into the computer file and just, you know, change the teams around a little."

"You mean hack into the school computer system?" Ronald sounded downright scandalized. "But that's completely unethical!"

"No, it's not," I argued quickly. "See, Lacey and I are like, um, two chemical formulas that don't go together. Or something. Anyway, the point is, we really shouldn't be near each other, especially on the same team. Otherwise we'll just end up fighting, and that could ruin the Olympics for everyone. So it's kind of your civic duty to help me out here. Otherwise the whole school will have to suffer the consequences."

I thought that sounded pretty convincing. I held my breath as Ronald mulled it over. "Hmmm," he said at last. "That makes sense. I guess."

"Does that mean you'll help me?" I demanded.

"I suppose so," Ronald agreed reluctantly.

"But only if you come over to my house tomorrow evening to assist."

I stared at the receiver. "Why?" I asked. "I
mean, I know my way around the Internet and
all that, but I'm totally clueless when it comes to
that programming stuff."

"That's the deal, Jessica," Ronald said firmly.
"Take it or leave it."

I frowned. Hanging out at Ronald's house definitely wasn't my idea of a fun way to spend a
perfectly good Friday night. Especially since I'd
been hoping to spend it with Damon.

I sighed. What choice did I have? "Fine. I'll be
there," I told him.

As I hung up, I comforted myself with the
thought that my plan was practically flawless.
All I had to do was survive one measly Friday-
night visit with Ronald, and all my problems
would be over. If Kristin wondered how the
teams got switched, I could just play dumb and
blame the computer. She knew there was no
way I'd be able to pull off something like this.

It would be the perfect crime.

Damon

I was heading for English class on Friday when I spotted Blue wandering down the hall ahead of me. As usual, he looked like he was strolling on the beach, not hurrying to class like the rest of us. Talk about a guy who's totally relaxed. I wish I could be that mellow.

"Blue!" I called. "Wait up."

"Hey, bro," Blue said, slapping me on the back as I caught up to him. "What's shakin'?"

"Not a lot," I replied. "But hey, I was just talking to Salvador and Brian. We were thinking about getting together for practice after school today."

The four of us had started a band called Big Noise. We weren't all that great yet—hence our name—but we were working on it.

Blue looked worried. "Sorry, dude," he said. "I can't make it."

"You can't?" I blinked in surprise. Blue doesn't exactly have an action-packed schedule. Basically he goes to school, hangs out with friends, and surfs. That's about it. "Why not?" I asked.

He shrugged. "I promised to give Elizabeth Wakefield surfing lessons."

I stared at him blankly, waiting for him to continue. "Why?" I prodded when it was clear he wasn't taking the hint.

"Oh, she's learning to ride the waves for a *Zone* article, and I'm the one who's teaching her," he said.

"Okay." I shrugged. "So can you do it another day? The ocean's always there, right?"

Blue was already shaking his head. "Can't do it, bro." He shrugged apologetically as we turned the corner and headed down the hall. "I promised."

I frowned, a little annoyed. "Look, Blue," I said. "There's other stuff I want to be doing this afternoon too. But the band has to take priority over girls, you know? At least for now, while we're still trying to get off the ground." Back when we'd first started the band, Salvador had gotten mad at us because we weren't really making any effort to get better. I'd thought he was overreacting, and maybe he was, but now I was starting to understand how he'd felt.

"I hear you, buddy. But this isn't about a girl. It's about *Zone*," Blue said earnestly. "Elizabeth and I have to get that article done. Deadlines, you know."

"Okay, I guess." I couldn't really argue with that. I was the only member of Big Noise who wasn't also on the *Zone* staff—writing isn't really my thing. But I'd heard all about it from Brian and Salvador, so I knew their deadlines were important.

It's a little weird that Blue's the only one worried about a deadline, though, I thought. *Brian and Salvador didn't say anything about working on stuff for Zone this weekend. So Blue's deadline can't be that tight, can it?*

I wasn't sure, but I didn't feel like getting into it. Arguing with Blue is kind of a lost cause— sort of like arguing with my little sister Kaia. Whatever you say, she just agrees with it and then does whatever she wants anyway.

"Okay," I said as we reached my classroom door. "So when are you going to be done with that? Maybe we could practice afterward."

Blue thought for a minute. "If you want, we could meet at the beach around five-thirty. I can hang around and practice as long as you want after that."

I winced. I'd been hoping to get together with Jessica later. Hanging out with her sounded like a much cooler way to spend Friday night than a band rehearsal with the guys. But what could I say? I'd just finished telling Blue that girls had to take a backseat to Big Noise, and I'd been the one to offer to meet him after his lesson with Elizabeth. Besides, maybe Jessica could come watch us or something. That way at least I'd get to see her.

"Deal," I said as the bell rang, making us both officially late for class. "I'll let the other guys know."

Note

Greetings, Jessica,

Are you still coming over to my house tonight? I should be finished eating dinner by seven-thirty. I have to be in bed by ten o'clock, so please arrive on time.

Sincerely,
Your locker partner,
Ronald R.

Note

Ronald,

Yes, I'm still coming. I said I was, didn't I???

And by the way, don't leave me any more notes!!!!!!!!!! Especially on the outside of our locker!!!

J.

Blue

"Okay," I said, leaning on my board. "There are two things you have to remember at all times."

"What are they?" Elizabeth asked, wriggling her fingers in the sand.

She was sitting on the beach with her legs stretched out in front of her, one sandal sort of flopping off her toes. She looked so totally cute that I sort of forgot what I was talking about. "Huh?" I said.

"You said there were two things I have to remember all the time," she said patiently.

"Oh! Yeah, that's right." I cleared my throat. *Chill*, I told myself. "Um, number one: You are the wave."

Elizabeth looked confused. "What do you mean?" she asked, glancing out at the surf.

"You are the wave," I repeated. "If you can feel it, you can ride it. Sort of a Zen thing, you know?"

"Um, okay." She bit her lip, still looking

slightly confused. But she nodded. "So what's number two?"

"Number two?" I was having trouble focusing again.

"You said there were two things to remember."

"Right." I was really going to have to get a grip, or Elizabeth was going to think I was a total loser. "Number two: Dude, the board is your best friend."

"Got it." This time she smiled, glancing at my trusty, battered old lucky surfboard.

I stood up straight and let the board fall flat onto the sand. "Okay. Let's talk about the stance." I was sort of getting into this now. I'd kind of shown Brian how to surf, but he was the only person I'd ever taught. I knew my lessons could use some improvement, so I changed them a bit for Elizabeth. Hopefully I'd made the lessons *better*, not just different.

Elizabeth watched as I stepped onto the board and planted my bare feet apart, pretending I'd just caught a really gnarly wave.

"Check it out. You've got to get some balance going, then keep it like this." Bending my knees and swaying back and forth, I demonstrated how to stay balanced while riding a wave. "Okay," I said after a minute, hopping off the board. "Want to give it a try?"

"Okay." Elizabeth stood up, kicked off her sandals, and brushed the sand off her legs. She stepped carefully onto the board, placing her feet exactly where mine had been. "How's this?"

"Huh?" I realized I was staring at her. She looked awesome there on my board. Like some kind of surf goddess. There was a little bit of a breeze, which made her blond hair dance around her face. The purple bathing suit she was wearing made her eyes look the same color as the ocean breakers behind her.

I shook my head, trying to shift my focus back to Elizabeth's surfing skills. This was getting a little crazy. For one thing, I was supposed to be teaching her the ways of the wave. For another, I'd liked Elizabeth since the day I met her—but crushing on her hadn't gotten me anywhere up until this point, and I didn't think it was going to get me anywhere now. Besides, I was pretty sure I wasn't her type.

"Blue, is something wrong?" Elizabeth shuffled her feet on the board, looking majorly anxious.

"Oh! No, sorry," I blurted out. "Uh, I was just thinking—I mean, nice suit."

She blushed, glancing down at herself. "This? Oh, it's, um—it's Jessica's, actually."

Right. Her twin. I always forgot she had one. "Well, it looks good with your eyes," I mumbled. "You know, uh, yours and Jessica's. Or whatever."

She seemed kind of embarrassed, though I wasn't sure why. She hadn't done anything goofy. I was the one who was staring at her like some kind of dork.

I felt my cheeks getting red. "Okay, here we go," I said, trying to sound businesslike. "Try putting your left foot a little farther back."

"You mean here?" Elizabeth moved her foot slightly.

I stepped forward. "A little farther." I poked her leg until she had it in the right spot. "Now, you have to sort of angle yourself and lean forward into the balance."

She looked confused. Taking a deep breath, I placed my hands on her waist to help her find the right stance on the board. As soon as I gave her a gentle push, though, she started totally cracking up.

I yanked my hands away. "What's wrong, dude?" I asked in alarm.

"S-S-Sorry," she replied between giggles. "Um, I mean, sorry about that. That tickled a little." She took a deep breath. "Go ahead."

"Uh, okay." I grabbed her by the waist again.

This time, as soon as my fingers touched the purple fabric of her bathing suit, she started laughing again. Her face was turning bright red, making her look kind of like a lobster. A cute lobster.

I pulled my hands away again, uncertain.

"Sorry, Blue," Elizabeth said breathlessly after a moment, when she finally had her laughter under control again. Her face was still looking pretty lobstery, though. "I'm really sorry about that. I guess I just—well, I'll show you."

Before I could react, she turned and started tickling me. "Whoa!" I shouted. I was so startled that I stepped backward and tripped over my own feet, sprawling flat on my back in the sand. Giggling wildly, Elizabeth came after me.

Okay, here's the deal. I'm totally ticklish. Always have been. Within seconds I was thrashing around on the sand, trying to escape her tickling fingers. At the same time I was doing my best to tickle her back. It wasn't easy since I was totally breathless from laughing so hard. Also, her long, blond hair was flying around and getting in my eyes, making it hard to see.

"Hi, guys," a voice said loudly from somewhere above us.

Elizabeth immediately stopped tickling me and toppled over. I glanced up, wiping tears of laughter from my eyes so I could see. *Huh? How did Elizabeth get up so fast?* She was staring down at me with a broad smile on her face.

No way, dude, I told myself, blinking to clear my head. Of course. Elizabeth was still on the sand beside me. *That's not her up there. That's Jessica.*

Elizabeth

I could feel my face turning bright red as I untangled myself from Blue and stood up. Jessica was staring at me with a curious look on her face. I could only imagine how this looked to her. "Um, hey," I greeted her, trying to sound casual. Like she caught me rolling around on the beach with a cute guy every day of the week. "What are you doing here?"

"Just thought I'd come down and catch some rays before the school-Olympics swim meet." Jessica held up her see-through vinyl beach bag. It contained sunglasses, tanning cream, and a couple of fashion magazines. A beach towel was slung over her shoulders. "By some horrible twist of fate, I ended up on the same team as Lacey." She grimaced as if that were the most revolting thing in the world. "I'm not setting foot in front of that girl in a bathing suit without a fierce tan. Even if we end up not— uh, I mean, so what are you doing here?"

I hardly heard what my twin was saying about the swim meet. I couldn't help being very aware of Blue, who had climbed to his feet and was standing next to me. Anyway, Jessica hadn't really answered my question. It was no huge surprise to find her hanging at the beach working on her tan. What I really wanted to know was, out of all the zillions of beaches in southern California, why did she have to pick Blue's beach?

"Um . . . what?" I said distractedly. Keeping my gaze on Jessica, I brushed some hair out of my eyes.

"I said, what are you two doing here?" Jessica asked innocently, putting a little too much emphasis on the words *you two.*

"Blue's teaching me to surf, remember?" I was irritated at her question. I'd told her all about our lessons and my article already. So why was she playing dumb?

"Oh. Of course." She was obviously trying to hide a grin. "Well, don't let me disturb you."

She turned away and started laying out her towel. I turned back to face Blue. "Um, so what's next?" I asked, trying to sound normal.

Blue shot Jessica a slightly nervous glance. I guess he was feeling a little weird about getting caught at our tickle fight too. I don't know what got into me—it's just that I kept laughing whenever he touched me, which was totally embarrassing. And I couldn't seem to control myself. All I could think of was to turn the tables and make him laugh too.

"Maybe you'll get the hang of the stance better if I just go ahead and show you instead of trying to make you do it," he said. "Here, check it out."

He hopped on the board again, demonstrating what he'd been talking about. I looked at him, but I was watching my twin out of the corner of my eye. Jessica was sitting on her towel, her sunglasses propped on her head as she unpacked her beach bag. She really looked like she was settling in for the afternoon. When she noticed me looking, she grinned and winked.

Great, I thought grimly, turning away. *Just what I need. An audience.*

Still, I reminded myself that it was really no big deal. Once Jessica saw that Blue and I were serious about our lesson—and our article—she'd lose any interest in watching us.

"Okay, got it?" Blue said, interrupting my thoughts.

"What?" I mumbled. "Oh, I mean, sure."

He nodded. "Now I'll go show you how it works out on the water. Just watch my stance, okay? Check out how I have to move around to stay balanced out there."

"I will." I smiled and waved as he tossed me a sloppy salute and loped down the beach, his lucky board tucked under his arm.

Jessica

I waited until Blue headed down to the water to demonstrate something or whatever he was supposed to be doing. As soon as he was out of hearing range, I turned to my twin with a smile.

"So, Liz," I said casually. "How's the lesson going? Looks to me like you're the teacher's pet."

She rolled her eyes. "Very funny. I already told you, Blue and I are just friends. Anyway, what made you come to this beach? You never come here."

I shrugged. "I'm supposed to meet Damon here. The guys are having a Big Noise practice tonight." I knew Elizabeth was trying to change the subject, but I wasn't about to let this Blue thing drop. "Look, Liz. You don't have to be embarrassed to admit it if you like Blue. I mean, he's not exactly my idea of a dream date, but hey—you've always had interesting taste in guys."

"Jess, Blue and I are just friends!" She folded

53

her arms across her chest. "Why won't you believe me?"

"Oh, Liz," I teased, wrapping my arm around her shoulders and ruffling her hair with my free hand. "It's okay if you have a *crush!* Tell your sister the truth!" Elizabeth, turning bright red, shrugged out of my grasp. I could tell she was trying not to laugh.

"You're driving me nuts! The truth is, Blue and I are friends," Elizabeth said firmly. "That's all. End of story."

I shrugged, picking up my bottle of sunscreen and rubbing it into my skin, then I checked my watch. There was still about an hour to go before Damon and the other guys arrived. I was already looking forward to their band rehearsal. Not that I was ever all that thrilled about hanging out with El Salvador. But it was a small price to pay to spend some time with Damon, especially since I wouldn't get to go out with him that night. I shuddered at the thought of what I was going to be doing instead.

Immediately banishing all thoughts of Ronald Rheece from my head, I returned my attention to my sister. She had turned to watch as Blue paddled out beyond the breakers and looked around, obviously searching for the perfect wave for his little demonstration.

"Look, Liz," I began. "I know it's always a little weird when you first like someone. You know, you're nervous, you're not sure if he likes you back. . . ."

"Argh!" Elizabeth threw her hands up in the air. "What is it going to take to convince you, Jess? I don't like Blue! I mean, I like him—as a friend. But I don't *like* like him."

I couldn't believe she was being so stubborn. Anyone with half an eye could see she was totally into Blue. If I'd had any doubt about that, their little tickle fest had definitely convinced me. "So let's say Blue started dating some amazing girl tomorrow," I said. "Are you telling me you wouldn't be the slightest bit jealous?"

"Of course not," Elizabeth replied stiffly. "I'd be happy for him. As a friend."

"Yeah, right." I rolled my eyes. I was sure that she was kidding herself, but before I could say so, Blue came jogging up the beach toward us, panting and dripping wet.

When he reached us, he tossed his head to shake the water out of his hair, sending droplets flying everywhere, even onto my beach towel. "Did you see that?" he asked Elizabeth breathlessly, tossing his surfboard onto the sand. That sent more droplets splashing over me.

"Um, yeah," she lied. "You looked great."

I couldn't help smirking. It was obvious that Elizabeth hadn't seen a second of his surfing run. "What did you think of that thing he did with his arms?" I asked casually. "Pretty cool, huh?"

Elizabeth glared at me. "Yes," she said through clenched teeth. "Incredible."

I grinned at her, then leaned back on my beach towel, leaving the two of them to continue their "lesson." If Elizabeth wanted to deny her own feelings, I figured I could live with it.

I flipped through my magazines for the next hour, glancing up occasionally to see how things were going. Elizabeth didn't get in the water at all, though Blue made her stand on the surfboard and sort of wiggle around a lot. He also went out and demonstrated a few more times. I had to admit, he really was a pretty awesome surfer.

I guess I must have drifted off for a few seconds. The next thing I knew, I was rudely awakened by cold water dripping on my head. I cracked open an eye. There was a shadow over me.

"Jessica?" Blue's voice said. "Do you have a watch?"

I opened my other eye and sat up. "What?" I asked, brushing the water drops off my forehead.

Blue was standing at the edge of my towel. Glancing past him, I saw Elizabeth holding his grubby old surfboard nearby.

"Sorry if I woke you, dude," Blue said. "I was just wondering what time it is."

I checked my watch. "It's five-twenty," I told him.

"Thanks, dude—er, Jessica." Blue shot me a goofy grin and then turned back toward Elizabeth. "Yo, it's almost time for the guys to get here," he told her, taking the board from her. "I guess we'd better call it quits for today."

"Oh. Okay." Elizabeth looked disappointed.

Blue kicked at the sand and shrugged. "Um, you can hang out and watch us rehearse if you want," he offered. "I mean, your sister's staying, right? It could be fun."

Elizabeth shot me a glance. "Thanks," she said quietly. "But I think I'd better get home. I want to make some notes for my article before dinner."

"Cool," Blue said, biting his lip. "I guess I'll catch you mañana, then."

I rolled my eyes. The two of them were so pathetic. Why couldn't they just admit they liked each other already? It was painfully obvious to the rest of the world. "Are you sure, Liz?" I asked, standing up and stretching. "There's still plenty of time before dinner."

57

"I'm sure." Elizabeth frowned at me, then turned away.

Whatever, I thought, flopping down on my towel again as Elizabeth gathered up her stuff. *If she wants to go home and sit in front of her computer instead of hanging out here at the beach with the guy she likes, it's her choice. Even though it's obvious that she'd rather stay.* I smiled as I flipped my sunglasses down from the top of my head. *A twin can always tell.*

Damon

"Check this out." Salvador struck a pose, flexing his biceps and doing a few quick dance steps on the sand. "Am I ready for prime time or what?"

Blue and Brian cracked up. I laughed too. Salvador is a real clown.

"Pretty cool, man," I said. "I bet MTV will be calling soon to offer us our own show."

Jessica snorted. She was watching us from her beach blanket, which was laid out on the sand at the edge of the area where we'd decided to practice that day. We didn't have our drum kit or anything, but we figured we could work on our moves and go over lyrics even without all our instruments and amps and stuff.

"Yeah, right," Jessica said, propping her elbows on her knees. "Boy band number 378, please take the stage!"

Salvador stuck out his tongue at Jessica, she rolled her eyes at him, and I started laughing. It's pretty funny—the two of them are always ragging on each other, but secretly, I think they like each other better than they'd ever admit.

My smile faded, though, as I realized that Jessica was actually right. We really did look like a reheated boy-band video most of the time. And there was nothing even remotely funny about that.

"Look, guys," I said. "Maybe we should talk about our image. Like, the fact that we don't have one."

"Damon's right." Brian spoke up, running one hand through his long, blond hair. "We don't want to be teenybopper rip-offs. We want to be trendsetters!"

"Cool," Blue said lazily. He was stretched out on the sand, his hands propped behind his head. "We'll be totally cutting edge."

"Not unless we figure out a way to stand out from the crowd," I pointed out. "There are tons of bands made up of guys like us out there."

Salvador shrugged. "That's it," he said. "Maybe that's our problem. We're all guys."

"Huh?" Blue blinked at him.

"Maybe we should get some girls into the band," Salvador said, looking excited. "We could use a bass player anyway. So maybe we should hold auditions and look for a cute *female* bass player."

"I don't know," I said dubiously. "I like Big

Noise the way it is. It would be kind of weird to start adding new members now."

Blue nodded. "I'm with you, bro," he said, glancing at me. "Having girls in the band would be a totally freaky vibe."

Salvador shrugged. "Fine," he said. "Do you guys have any better ideas?"

"Let's think about it," I said. "We need something to make people notice us. Something totally different. What could we do?"

Brian bit his lip. "I don't know. I guess we could come up with, like, costumes or something."

"Yeah!" Jessica giggled. "You could all dress up in pink ostrich feathers!" Everyone laughed, but only halfheartedly. "Seriously, though, I hate to admit it," Jessica said, glancing at Salvador, "but I think El Salvador is right."

Salvador staggered back, clutching at his heart. "*What* was that?" He gasped dramatically. "I would have sworn I just heard Jessica Wakefield agree with me!"

"There's a first time for everything," Jessica muttered. "But seriously, I think a girl bass player would really add a lot to the band."

Salvador narrowed his eyes suspiciously. "Wait a minute," he said. "You're not volunteering, are you?"

"Ha-ha." Jessica rolled her eyes. "I stink at

anything musical. But I'm sure if you held auditions, plenty of girls would want to try out." She smiled at me. "Don't you think that would be cool?"

I can never resist Jessica when she shoots me that amazing smile. "Well . . . ," I began. I glanced at the other guys. "I guess it could work. It might even improve our sound."

Brian still looked uncertain. "Maybe," he agreed reluctantly.

I looked over at Blue. "Yo, if that's what you guys want, I'm in," he said.

Jessica smiled, looking satisfied. "Good, then that's settled," she said briskly. "When are you going to hold the auditions?"

"Why wait?" I shrugged. "We could do it this weekend."

Blue cleared his throat. "This weekend?" he repeated. "Uh, that's not really cool for me. You know, schedulewise. How about next Sunday?"

"No way," Salvador exclaimed. "We've got to move on this sooner than that. Our fans are waiting!"

"Well, I agree we shouldn't sit around until next weekend," Brian said. "But we should give people a few days' notice. We need time to get the word out."

"I could make up a poster if you want," Blue offered.

"Excellent," I said, glancing over at Jessica. She

was smiling happily. It made me feel pretty good to know she was taking such an interest in Big Noise. At first she'd acted kind of surprised that I'd wanted to be in the band so much. But now she seemed cool with it. "Let's make the auditions next week. How's Monday for everybody?"

"Fine with me," Brian said.

"Monday's cool," Salvador agreed.

Blue nodded. "Okay, then," he said. "I'll put Monday on the poster."

Jessica

"See you later," I called to my parents, who were in the den, watching the news. "I'll be back by curfew."

"Hold it!" My dad looked up, hitting the mute button on the remote. "Where are you going?"

I grimaced. The last thing I wanted to do was announce where I was headed, but what could I say? "Um, to Ronald Rheece's," I admitted, trying to sound as casual as possible.

"Really?" Mom looked skeptical. "I thought you weren't crazy about Ronald."

"Yeah, well, he's okay. He's helping me with some computer stuff for school." That was *kind* of the truth.

"Schoolwork? On a Friday night?"

"You know me." I grinned weakly. "I live for school."

Mom snorted at that, and Dad rolled his eyes. "Right. Well, just be home by curfew," Mom said, turning back to the TV. "And be sure to say hi to Ronald's parents for us."

Jessica

Out in the garage I grabbed my bike. It was a pretty long ride to Ronald's house, but there was no way I was going to ask anyone in my family to drive me there. My parents would get all goofy about it—they know Ronald's family, and they're always trying to tell me what a wonderful young man he is. As for my older brother, Steven, he would probably laugh so hard, he'd give himself a cramp.

I wheeled my bike down the driveway, then climbed on and headed toward the end of the block. At least this evening wouldn't be a total waste. The ride over there and back would help me get in shape for Olympics week.

As I rode, my mind wandered back to the Big Noise rehearsal. I smiled as I imagined what Elizabeth would say when she heard about the plan to bring a girl into the band.

It'll be the perfect way to help her figure out how she really feels about Blue, I thought, my legs pumping steadily. *When she starts feeling jealous about her nonboyfriend hanging out with a rock-and-roll chick, she'll finally have to face up to the fact that she really likes Blue.*

It wasn't that I wanted Elizabeth to feel bad. Of course not. But if she never faced her true feelings, she'd never do anything about them. I mean, Elizabeth isn't the most aggressive person when it comes to boys, so sometimes she needs an extra push in the right direction. And that push was going to come from me. Helping her and Blue get together was practically my sisterly duty.

Ronald answered the door when I arrived. "Jessica!" he said with a big grin. "Come right in. Make yourself at home."

"Thanks," I muttered, darting into the house before anyone could happen by and see me there. I had no intention of making myself at home. All I wanted to do was get the Lacey thing over with and get out of there.

"Hi, Jessica," a voice called from the other room.

"Hi, Mrs. Rheece," I hollered. "My parents said to tell you hello."

"How are they doing?" Mrs. Rheece replied.

"Fine," I said. "They're . . ." But before I could say anything else, Ronald started dragging me toward the stairs.

"Come up to my room," he said. "We'll use my computer. I have a cable modem."

He looked very proud of himself for some reason, so I forced a smile. "That's cool," I said as I followed him upstairs. "So what do you need me to do?"

Ronald didn't answer. He just gestured for me

J e s s i c a

to follow as he reached the top of the stairs and headed for a doorway at the end of the hall. I shrugged and followed.

I wrinkled my nose as I stepped into Ronald's room. It was pretty much exactly what I would have expected. Model airplanes hung from the ceiling. There was a large, complicated-looking contraption on a table near the window, which I guessed must be one of the ham radios he was always blabbing about. A huge poster of Einstein hung over the bed. And to top it all off, he had Star Trek sheets.

"The computer's over here." Ronald walked over to a large desk. A messy bulletin board hung over it, filled with all sorts of scribbled mathematical formulas, a few A-plus test papers, and an autographed photo of Mr. Spock.

"Okay, let's get to work," I said, more than a little weirded out. If anyone had told me a week ago that I'd ever voluntarily enter Ronald Rheece's bedroom, I would have told them they were crazy. "What do we do first?"

"You can sit over there." Ronald gestured vaguely at a chair. Meanwhile he sat down at the desk and hit a couple of buttons on the computer. It bleeped and started to boot up. "I'll take care of the computer part. It shouldn't be too difficult."

I frowned. "Okay, then why exactly am I here?"

Ronald shrugged, keeping his eyes trained on the computer monitor. "Oh, well, I guess, um . . ."

"Ronald!" I said warningly. "What's going on? Why did you drag me over here if you can do this all by yourself?"

He glanced at me with a sheepish grin. "I suppose you could call it curiosity," he admitted. "I must say, I'm quite mystified by the dynamic between two girls that could necessitate such extreme measures, and I can't help wondering if it might have something to do with Darwinian principles."

I blinked. "Uh, English translation, please?"

"I don't get why you and Lacey hate each other so much," he clarified.

"Oh." I was sorry I'd asked. "Let's just say we don't see eye to eye on most things. Like life, for instance."

He nodded earnestly. "Yes, but why? From my observations during the time period directly after you enrolled at SVJH, I was under the impression that you and Lacey were becoming friends. So what happened to reverse that process?"

Aha! I was starting to get it. Ronald Rheece— the same guy who resided in a stratosphere so far outside the loop that it wasn't visible to the naked eye—wanted the dirt. Plain and simple.

I frowned slightly. The last thing I felt like doing was explaining to Ronald how Lacey had used me and dissed me one too many times, back when I still thought I wanted her as my friend. How she had made me feel completely unwelcome in my new school when it was so important to me to fit in. And how she was so totally threatened by the fact that Kristin and I were friends that she would do or say just about anything to get my goat.

Still, I didn't really have much choice. I had to keep Ronald happy if I wanted him to change those teams for me. Besides, who would he tell? It wasn't like he had any friends outside the math club, and they all talked only to one another.

"Okay," I said with a sigh. "It's like this. . . ."

Elizabeth Wakefield's
Top-Five Requirements for a
~~Cute~~ Practical Swimsuit

1. Should be streamlined and sturdy—good for surfing
2. Must be more sophisticated looking than my dumb old purple one
3. Two-piece??? Or do surfer girls only wear one-piece???
4. Should not ride up in heavy surf
5. Must look good with my eyes

Elizabeth

The morning after my first surfing lesson I decided it was time to hit the mall for some serious bathing-suit shopping. If I was going to be a surfer girl, I had to look the part, right? Besides, I'd already told Blue my old purple suit was Jessica's, mostly because I'd noticed it had a big stain on the stomach and a few loose threads on the shoulder. Yes, it was definitely time for a new beach look. And I had only a few hours before it was time for my next lesson. I had to make the most of my shopping time.

I brought the cordless phone into my room and called Anna to see if she wanted to come with me. "I could use a second opinion," I told her, leaning back in my desk chair. "It's so hard to tell how bathing suits really look, especially under those horrible fluorescent lights they always have in dressing rooms."

"Sorry, Liz," Anna said. "I'm just on my way out to meet Toby."

"Really?" I raised one eyebrow in interest. Anna was getting pretty tight with Toby, this really cute

73

guy she met in drama club. They weren't exactly boyfriend-girlfriend yet, but they'd been spending an awful lot of time together lately. And she couldn't go more than two sentences without mentioning his name. "Is this a date?"

She giggled sheepishly, but I could tell she was really happy. "I don't know," she said. "Well, maybe. Larissa was supposed to come too, but now she can't make it. So I guess it's just the two of us. We're going to this improv festival over in Smithville. You should come with us if you want."

"Oh. That sounds like fun. But I've really got to find a suit." I swallowed a sigh, realizing that this meant I was on my own. "Have a great time."

I hung up and dropped the phone on my desk, wondering what to do now. Just then Jessica wandered into my room.

"Hi," she said, flopping down on my bed. "I'm bored."

I blinked. Of course! How could I have forgotten? I had my very own expert shopper right there in my very own house. Namely, my shopaholic twin sister.

"Want to go to the mall?" I asked eagerly.

Jessica shrugged. "Maybe," she said. "What are you shopping for?"

I hesitated. "Um, nothing in particular," I hedged. "I just thought we could browse. You know, check out some cute clothes or whatever."

"Cute clothes for what?" Jessica pressed, looking a little dubious.

"You know, just cute clothes," I answered innocently.

"Oh, really? Well, if you don't have a specific goal in mind, I'm not interested." With that, she got up and walked out into the hallway.

I hurried after her and dragged her back into my room. "Okay, okay. Here's the thing. I, well, I'm going to be in that surfing competition next week, like I told you. So I figured I should probably get a new bathing suit."

"Aha!" Jessica smirked. "So you want something cute to wear to your next lesson with Blue, huh?"

I frowned. "Very funny," I snapped. "This has nothing to do with Blue. We're just friends, remember? Anyway, I just want to find a suit that will be up to the rigors of surfing. It's not as easy as it looks, you know."

"Ri-i-i-ght," Jessica said with a grin. "If you say so. I'm sure we can find you something totally rigorous. Let's go!"

As soon as we entered the mall, Jessica turned into a shopping whirlwind. She must have made me try on fifty different suits, all sorts of colors and styles. I just did what she said, peeling off one and slipping into another as fast as I could. Most of them didn't work for one reason or another—

they didn't fit quite right, the color was wrong for me, or they just weren't my style. But there were a few I really liked. Including this adorable daisy-print one-piece with spaghetti straps.

Hmmm, I thought, twisting and turning in front of the mirror as I checked it out. Jessica was off searching the racks for more prospects, so I had a few minutes to examine it. *This one's really pretty cute. I wonder if Blue would like it.*

I stopped cold, running that last sentence back in my head. *If Blue would like it?* Why should I care so much if Blue would like it? He was my friend—he would be fine with anything I wore, just like Anna or Salvador or any of my other friends.

Unless maybe I really am starting to think of him as more than a friend, I thought uncertainly. *Maybe I do care a little bit what he thinks of the way I look. Maybe that's part of the reason I want a new bathing suit.*

I frowned and shook my head. *No way.* Blue wasn't anything like me. We had almost nothing in common, and I was *sure* I wasn't his type. So what would be the point of liking him anyway? There was no point, and it didn't matter because I *didn't* like him in that way. All of Jessica's little comments were just starting to get to me. She was making a big deal out of nothing as usual, and it was making me feel weird.

That was all there was to it. Definitely.

Jessica

Elizabeth must have tried on every single bathing suit at the mall. For a while she was leaning toward this icky flower-print one, but I finally convinced her to go with the adorable silvery green one I found at my favorite store.

"I'm sure Blue—I mean, your surfing instructor—will think it looks very, um, rigorous," I assured her as we left the store, trying to keep from smiling. After this whole bathing-suit thing, I was more sure than ever that Elizabeth had it bad for Blue. I mean, I could totally identify. When Damon and I first started going out, I always wanted to look perfect whenever I saw him. I don't worry about that kind of stuff with him so much anymore.

But it *was* a little surprising coming from Elizabeth. She's not usually the flirty, dress-up type. The thing is, Elizabeth has always been kind of weird when it comes to guys. It took her about a million years to admit she liked her first boyfriend back at our old middle school. And then this year she and El Salvador had some sort of weird romantic vibe going. They never ended up going out, though. Thank goodness.

"That's not the point," Elizabeth said primly. "And you know it."

"Whatever." I didn't want to argue about it anymore. Anyway, when Big Noise held their auditions, we'd see who was "just friends."

Elizabeth checked her watch. "Oops, it's later than I realized," she said. "I'd better get home and change, or I'll be late for my lesson."

I checked my own wrist before I realized I'd forgotten to put on my watch that morning. It didn't matter, though. Being at the mall had put me in a good mood and I wasn't quite ready to pack it in for the day yet. "Go ahead," I told my twin. "I think I'll hang out here for a while."

"Okay. See you later." Elizabeth turned away. Then she stopped and smiled at me over her shoulder. "And Jess—thanks." She hurried off, clutching her shopping bag, before I could respond.

I turned and strolled down the mall, glancing into the windows of the stores. The food court was just ahead, so I decided to go get a soda. I headed over to Taco Wacko and placed my order.

As I was ditching my straw paper in the nearest trash can, someone called my name. I looked over to see a tall, red-haired girl waving to me from a table nearby. I waved back and headed toward her. "Hey, Susie," I said when I reached her table. "What's up?"

"Not much." Susie Williams had been transferred to SVJH from our old middle school at the beginning of eighth grade, just like me and Elizabeth and some others. "How about you? How's track going?"

I hardly heard the question. I'd just glanced down at Susie's table. She was eating a plate of french fries and reading a magazine. A music magazine. At that, my mind bounced straight back to Elizabeth and Blue.

"You used to be in a band, right?" I blurted out.

Susie blinked. "Uh, yeah," she said, picking up a fry and dipping it in her little paper cup of ketchup. "Why?"

"Just wondering," I said, taking in her wild auburn waves, concert T-shirt, and black jeans and boots. Definitely cute rock-chick material. "You don't play bass by any chance, do you?"

"I mostly play guitar." Susie shrugged. "But I've jammed on the bass a few times, just for fun."

"Perfect!" I grinned. "Then I've got great news for you." I quickly told her all about the Big

Noise auditions. I didn't exactly tell her it was mostly a bunch of guys goofing off and pretending to be rock stars. I kind of made it sound like they were just weeks away from being the next big hit on MTV.

Susie listened with interest, chewing on a fry. "Wow," she said when I finished. "Sounds pretty cool. I was just thinking it would be fun to get back into playing more seriously again."

"This could be the perfect chance to do it!" I assured her.

"Cool." Susie smiled.

I smiled back, but I was a little distracted. I'd just spotted Lacey. She was hanging out with a couple of older girls over near the pizza counter, laughing and staring at the chubby teenage guy who was working there.

I grimaced. Talk about a mood killer. Suddenly the mall didn't seem like such a great place to be anymore. Not that I was afraid of Lacey or anything, but I really didn't want to deal with her just then if I could help it.

"Um, I just remembered; I have to go," I told Susie hurriedly. "But don't forget—Monday afternoon."

"I'll be there," she promised. "Thanks for the tip, Jessica."

"No problem." With a quick wave I took off for the mall exit.

But even seeing Lacey wasn't enough to totally kill my good mood. *Talk about a busy weekend,* I thought with a secret smile as I stepped out of the mall into the warm midday sunshine. *Not only did I figure out the perfect plan to head off an Olympics-week disaster, but I also managed to set up a little something to kick start Liz's love life. Now all I have to do is sit back and watch it all unfold.*

Blue

"Excellent!" I shouted, cupping my hands so Elizabeth could hear me. "You're totally a natural!"

She grinned, then returned her attention to her board. Well, technically it was *my* board, but whatever. It was our second day of lessons, and Elizabeth was finally in the water, trying out all the tips I'd given her. I was standing on the beach so I could get a good view of her technique.

I watched as she tugged at her wrist strap to pull the board toward her. She picked it up and jogged toward me through the surf. Her blond hair was plastered to her head, she had sand on her knees, and one strap of her bathing suit was crooked, but she still looked cute.

"Was that really okay?" she asked breathlessly. "I mean, I thought I had it this time, but then I started to wobble. . . ."

I gave her a thumbs-up. "More than okay, dude," I told her. "It was awesome."

"Thanks." She seemed psyched about the

compliment. "Surfing's a lot harder than I realized. But it's a lot of fun too."

"Tell me about it." I glanced out at the ocean. "We've only got a few more minutes until the tide changes and the waves get lame. Want to give it one more try before then?"

"Sure," Elizabeth agreed. She hoisted her board. "Any last-minute tips this time?"

I shrugged and grinned. "Just to remember two things—you are the wave, and—"

"I know, I know." She cut me off with a laugh. "The board's my best friend, dude."

She jogged back into the water. I sat down on the sand and watched as she hopped the first few lines of waves. They were already getting smaller. Yep, it was just about time to pack it in for the afternoon.

Before long Elizabeth was swimming, holding on to the board and kicking her way over the bigger swells out past the breakers. She paddled around for a minute or two, watching for just the right wave to come along. Just like I'd taught her.

She really is catching on, I thought, stretching out my legs. The sand felt warm and comfortable beneath them. *And I'm not just saying that because she's—*

"Uh-oh," I muttered aloud.

I'd just spotted something. Elizabeth had spun around to face shore—a stray current must have caught the board and turned it. That was no biggie in itself. But it meant that she couldn't see what was behind her—a big wave, bigger than it should have been that time of day, was swelling up and coming at her.

"Yo!" I shouted, jumping to my feet and cupping my hands around my mouth. "Elizabeth! Look out!"

A few people on the beach nearby looked at me strangely, but I hardly noticed. Elizabeth was staring my way, but I wasn't sure if she'd heard me.

I didn't even realize I was running toward her until I felt the cool ocean water splashing around my ankles. I raced through the shallows, then dove as soon as the water was deep enough. When I resurfaced, I could see that Elizabeth had finally managed to turn around—just in time to see the wave starting to break over her.

I kept my head out of the water as I swam, watching as she paddled desperately, trying to keep enough ahead of the big wave to catch it with her board. But it was too late. Just as she started to climb up on the board, the wave broke, flinging her off and dragging her under.

85

Uh-oh, I thought grimly. *Wipeout.*

Swimming as fast as I could, I ducked just in time as my board went flying past, almost conking me on the skull. A second later I saw Elizabeth's blond head pop up. She sputtered and coughed.

"Hold on!" I shouted, almost taking in a mouthful of salt water myself. "I'm coming."

Seconds later I reached her, just as another, smaller wave lifted us both up. I grabbed her around the shoulders, helping her keep her head above water.

She coughed again, then made a weird sound.

"Are you okay?" I asked as I started pulling her toward shore. "Are you crying? Uh, or laughing?"

"I—I'm not sure," she choked out. "Both, I think."

She seemed to think that was pretty funny because this time I'm almost sure she was laughing. I held on to her and kicked off toward shore, glancing over my shoulder to make sure there were no more surprise monster waves coming.

Elizabeth's shoulders shook as she continued to laugh and cough at the same time. Tears were mixing with the ocean water on her face. I was a little worried, but when we reached solid ground, she stood up and walked the rest of the way to dry sand with no trouble, dragging my board behind her. I made Elizabeth sit down on it to catch her breath.

"Are you sure you're okay?" I asked. "That was a pretty scary wave."

She nodded, letting out a hiccup. "I'm fine," she said. "I mean, it was a little scary, I guess. But not terrifying."

"Whoa." I looked at her with respect. "You're pretty brave."

She shrugged. "Not really," she said, glancing down at her toes. "I think it was just because I knew you were here, looking out for me. It made me feel safe."

I wasn't quite sure how to answer that one. It made me feel a little strange—sort of happy and queasy at the same time.

"Cool," I said at last. Then I went to get her a towel.

Instant Messages

ANA3:   Hey, Liz, you there?

wkfldE: I'm here. How was your "date" w/ Toby?

ANA3:   Excellent!!! :-) How was yours with Blue?

wkfldE: Ha-ha, funny. It wasn't a date, and U know it.

ANA3:   R U sure? Heh heh.

wkfldE: Give it a rest. Blue & I R just friends!

ANA3:   I know, I know. Kidding.

wkfldE: Sorry. So Toby?

ANA3:   Toby is *so amazing!* I can talk with him for hours and never get bored. Every girl should have a guy like that, don't U think?

wkfldE: Yeah, definitely.

ANA3:   Who knows, that guy might already be right in front of your big BLUE eyes.

wkfldE: Ugh!

Jessica

On Sunday, Elizabeth spent about an hour in the bathroom, getting ready for her next "lesson," aka date, with Blue. Finally the door from the bathroom into my room opened, and she stepped out.

"Does this shirt match?" she asked.

I glanced up from the magazine I was reading. She was wearing the bathing suit I'd picked out for her, with an oversized, gauzy lavender shirt over it. "It looks fine," I said, sitting up on my bed. "So you have another lesson today, huh." I did my best not to smirk when I said "lesson."

"Yeah," Elizabeth said, checking herself out in the mirror. "I've got to get in all the practice I can. The competition's in less than a week, you know."

"Right." I kept my voice as casual as possible. "Does that mean you were planning on going over there tomorrow after school?"

"Uh-huh." Elizabeth was still staring at herself, fiddling with the straps on her bathing suit.

"Hmmm. That's weird. I thought he'd be busy with other things."

She shot me a suspicious look in the mirror. "What other things?"

I shrugged. "Oh, didn't Blue mention it?" I said, pasting my most innocent expression on my face. "Big Noise decided to hold tryouts tomorrow after school. They're looking for a new bass player." I waited a beat. "A *girl* bass player," I added.

Elizabeth turned around and frowned at me. "Really? Are you sure?"

"Absolutely," I assured her. "Blue even offered to make up the poster for it. They're looking for a talented, hip rocker chick to spice up their image. I'm surprised he didn't mention it."

"Oh. Well, we were pretty busy yesterday." Elizabeth shrugged. "I guess he forgot."

"Maybe," I said. "Anyway, who knows? This could be Blue's chance to find that amazing girl I was talking about the other day. Remember? I could totally see him hitting it off with a fellow musician."

"Good. I hope he does," Elizabeth said blandly, though a little crease had appeared in her forehead, like she was trying to hold back a frown. She was obviously trying to pretend what I was saying didn't bother her. But I could tell it did.

Good, I thought, lying back on my bed and smiling at the ceiling as she hurried out of my room, mumbling something about being late. *It's only a matter of time before Liz faces the truth.*

Blue

"How's this?" Elizabeth balanced on my surfboard, which was propped up on a pile of sand. I was teaching her how to cope if a wave got tricky and tried to tip her.

"Pretty good," I said thoughtfully, rubbing my chin. "But can you hold your position when I do—this?" At that, I jumped forward and started tickling her.

She slapped my hands away. "Quit it!" she snapped, quickly stepping off the board away from me.

"What's the matter?" I was surprised by her attitude. She sounded downright peeved. "I was just kidding around."

Elizabeth frowned. "Sorry. It's just that I have a lot of work to do if I don't want to make a total fool of myself on Saturday." Her voice had this chilly sort of edge to it. "Now, come on—let's get back to work."

"Uh, okay. Whatever." I shrugged. "Why don't you go out and try a run? I'll watch."

"All right." Her voice still sounded weird—kind of formal, like I was an actual teacher instead of just a dude showing her how to surf. I was getting some flashbacks to the days when Elizabeth first joined the volleyball team my friend Rick and I are on. She'd been totally intense—like, obsessed with winning.

This is probably more of the same, I thought, watching as she picked up my board and headed for the water, her chin sort of jutting forward with concentration. *She's a lot more intense than I am about most stuff—it's just her thing, like it or not.*

I sighed, figuring all I could do was try to be understanding. But I had to admit, it was bumming me out a little. I'd thought she'd learned her lesson, figured out that life was more fun when you just mellowed out some.

Oh, well, I thought, squinting into the sun as I watched her paddle out over the breakers. *She got over the volleyball attitude thing after a while. I guess she'll probably get over this too.*

Jessica

"Hey, I forgot to ask you," Damon said. "What did you end up doing Friday night?"

I gulped, glancing around the crowded SVJH hallway. It was Monday morning before first period, and Damon and I were hanging at his locker. I thought about telling him the truth, but I didn't want a big lecture from him about trying to get along with Lacey. "Um, just some lame family stuff," I mumbled. "Anyway, are you psyched about the Big Noise tryouts today?"

"Sure, I guess." Damon leaned against the metal locker. "I just hope Blue remembered to hang up his poster. We want to have as many people as we can get to choose from."

At that moment I spotted a familiar face heading toward us. "You can ask him yourself," I told Damon. "Here he comes now."

"Yo, dudes," Blue greeted us as he reached us. "What's shakin'?"

As usual, he looked like some kind of character from one of those lame old Beach Boys songs my

93

dad was always listening to. He was wearing baggy, fluorescent green shorts, a T-shirt with some kind of hideous surfing logo on it, and big, clunky sandals. His blond hair was sticking up in all directions, as if he hadn't bothered to glance into a mirror as he rolled out of bed.

What's the big deal about him anyway? I wondered, shaking my head as Blue and Damon performed some sort of complex high-five-type greeting. *I just don't get it. Liz definitely has the weirdest taste in guys.*

In any case, it really wasn't important whether I thought Blue was boyfriend material or not. The only important thing was that my twin liked him. Even if she wouldn't admit that yet.

"So how are the surfing lessons going, Blue?" I asked casually. "Are you guys having fun?"

To my surprise, he hesitated before answering. "Uh, yeah, I guess," he said at last. "I mean, it's totally fun. Except that lately Elizabeth seems to be taking the whole thing kind of seriously. You know, she's, like, intense." He shrugged. "I was thinking about it, and I guess maybe she's stressed. You know, because of her *Zone* article. And the competition. She wants to do well on both of them, and it's getting her down. Or something."

I coughed to hide a laugh. Coming from Blue, that was practically a psychological case study. *Sounds like he's been thinking about Elizabeth almost as much as she's been thinking about him,* I thought.

That reminded me. "Hey, I almost forgot," I told Damon and Blue. "I ran into my friend Susie Williams over the weekend. She's this totally awesome musician—she's been playing the bass practically since she was born. I bet she'll be perfect for Big Noise. Anyway, I told her about the auditions, and she's going to be there."

"Cool," Damon said with a smile. "Thanks, Jessica."

He looked so adorable when he smiled—it made me want to laugh out loud. Or sing or something. I settled for just smiling back.

"Yeah," Blue broke in, spoiling the moment. "Totally, Jessica. We'll definitely remember you when we're rich and famous."

I rolled my eyes. "Yeah, right," I said. "Just get through this audition stuff first, okay? Then you can start writing your Grammy acceptance speech."

"So where do you want to meet this afternoon?" Damon asked Blue. "I figure we should try to agree on what kind of a bass player we're looking for while we're walking over to your place."

Blue wet his lips and glanced around the hall, looking sort of nervous. "Um, I was going to talk to you about that, bro," he said. "I don't think I can be there. You know, for the tryouts."

"What?" Damon frowned. "What do you mean? We all have to be there. We agreed, remember?"

"I know." Blue cleared his throat. "It's just that I'm supposed to have another lesson with Elizabeth after school. It's totally okay, though, dude—you can still have the tryouts at my place. Leaf will let you in."

I glanced up at Damon's face. He did *not* look pleased. He was scowling at Blue. "Come on, man," he said sternly. "This is important. We can't slack off now, or we might as well just forget the whole thing."

It was amazing. Damon even looked cute when he was angry. Well, as long as he wasn't angry at *me*. "Damon's right," I told Blue. "Elizabeth will get over it if you miss one measly lesson."

"But dude, she's supposed to be in the surfing competition this weekend," Blue protested. "She needs to practice."

"So find someone else to help her." Damon crossed his arms over his chest. "You're not the only surfer in southern California, you know."

"Yeah, I'll substitute teach for you if you want," I put in with a grin, imagining my twin's reaction if she saw me walking across the beach with a surfboard instead of Blue. "Liz and I can have a total surfin' safari."

"I'm telling you, man," Damon said grimly. "You've got to figure something out."

Blue sighed, glancing from me to Damon. "All right, bro," he said. "I guess you're right. I'll be at the tryouts this afternoon." He shrugged. "I can ask my bud Rick to pinch-hit for me with Elizabeth."

Big Noise Auditions
Monday Afternoon

3:42 P.M.   Blue, Damon, Salvador, and Brian meet in the school parking lot and start walking toward Blue's house. Damon wonders how many people will show up at the auditions. "Are you kidding?" Sal says. "This is the chance of a lifetime. We'll be totally mobbed!"

3:46 P.M.   As the other guys continue to talk about the auditions, Blue sneaks a peek at his watch, wondering if Elizabeth is on her way to the beach yet. For the fifteenth time he wishes he'd had a chance to talk to Elizabeth before school let out. She won't even know he's not teaching her today until Rick shows up at the beach and explains that he's filling in.

3:50 P.M.   The guys arrive at Blue's place. They head into the garage and start setting up. Blue checks his watch again.

4:05 P.M.   Brian begins to worry because no one has shown up yet to audition. "Chill out, bro," Blue says. "You know how these musician types are. They'll be here."

4:07 P.M.   Blue thinks how lucky Rick is to be hanging out with Elizabeth while he's stuck in his garage with a bunch of guys.

4:26 P.M.   "It's been almost half an hour," Damon points out, leaning back against an amplifier. "Where is everyone?"

4:32 P.M.   "Maybe we should go over a couple of songs or something," Brian suggests. Blue just kicks at a squashed aluminum soda can on the garage floor, pretending it's a hacky sack.

4:55 P.M.   Big Noise has finished playing all of their songs. "Blue, you did put today's date on the poster, didn't you?" Brian asks. Blue nods.

4:59 P.M.   Still nobody has showed up for the auditions. Damon peers out the garage door like a sailor searching for land. Nearby, Brian picks at a scab on his elbow while Salvador sings "Yankee Doodle" to himself. Blue sighs.

5:08 P.M.   "This is ridiculous," Damon says abruptly, standing up. "Nobody's going to show. We might as well pack it in and stop sitting around wasting our time." Blue checks his watch, feeling a sudden surge of hope. If he hurries, maybe—just maybe . . .

5:13 P.M. Blue arrives at the beach, breathless from running. He scans the people hanging on the sand and playing in the waves, but Elizabeth and Rick are nowhere to be seen. Bummer.

Flyer

Yo, Female Bass Players!

BIG NOSE wants to give you your big break!

Are you as talented as Britney Spears, as cool as Elvis, and as beautiful as Elizabeth ~~Wakefield~~ Taylor?

If that sounds like you, this hot local band wants to see what you can do. Come on down and show us your stuff on Monday afternoon at 4:00 in Blue Spiccoli's garage. He's in the book.

Rock on!

Blue

The next morning I was still majorly bummed out about the lame auditions. I couldn't believe I'd wasted the whole afternoon when I could have been with Elizabeth. I wasn't going to make that mistake again, that was for sure. If the guys wanted to reschedule the auditions, they would just have to wait until after the surfing competition.

When I got to my locker, I found Damon there, waiting for me. He had a large piece of cardboard tucked under his arm. "Yo, dude," I greeted him with a yawn. "What's up?"

Damon held up the cardboard, and I saw that it was the poster I'd made for the auditions. "This," he snapped.

I blinked, noticing for the first time that he seemed kind of uptight. "What's the matter?" I shrugged. "I know, I know—I probably should've put up more than just the one poster. But I figured since it was right there in the Cue Café window, everybody would see it."

For some reason, that didn't seem to make him feel any better. He waved the poster at me again. "You're supposed to be the big writer now, right?" he fumed. "So didn't you even bother to proofread this before you hung it up?"

"What do you mean?" I was getting some seriously bad vibes from him now. "What's wrong, bro?"

Damon pointed. "Read this," he demanded.

I shrugged, deciding to humor him. "'Big Noise wants to give you your big break,'" I read.

"Wrong," he cut me off. "Try again."

"'Big Noise—' Oops." I gulped, suddenly noticing the problem. "Uh, 'Big *Nose* wants to give you your big break.'"

"Right," Damon said grimly. "Big Nose. No wonder nobody showed up yesterday—everyone who saw this sign probably thought it was a big joke. Who names their band Big Nose?"

I groaned. He was totally right, and I knew it. "Sorry, bro," I said. "I guess I was in kind of a hurry when I was making it. You know, I wanted to get it up fast so lots of people would see it." And so I could go back to thinking about Elizabeth, of course. I didn't mention that last part to Damon, though.

"Whatever," Damon muttered. He stared at the poster. "Where'd you come up with 'as beautiful as Elizabeth Taylor' anyway? She's, like, old."

"Yeah, I know. But dude, she was pretty hot back in the day. I've seen some of her movies on cable." I shrugged weakly, not wanting to admit the real reason. I'd written Elizabeth Wakefield's name first, and it was easier to write over one name than two.

"Whatever." Damon gave me a look of general annoyance. I could tell he wasn't ready to let this go yet. "The point is, the auditions were a total bust."

"Sorry," I said again. "You're right; it's so totally my bad. I guess I'm just kind of distracted this week. You know, what with that *Zone* article and all. . . ."

Damon sighed. Ripping the poster in half, he tossed it toward a nearby trash can. "Blue, don't take this the wrong way, man," he said. "But you gotta start focusing on something other than Elizabeth Wakefield for a change."

Note

Hey, Ronald!

Did you hear? Mr. Todd is going to announce the school-Olympics teams tomorrow! So I just thought I'd better check and make extra, double, super-duper sure that everything is all fixed. You know what I mean.

Let me know!

J.

Note #2

Ronald,
  What's going on? Didn't you get my other note?
  In case you didn't, I just need to know that we're
all set. You know, with the plan.
                                    Jessica

Note #3

Hello???!!!???
   Earth to Ronald!
   Did you get my other notes or what? I need to know what's going on!!!!!!!!!

                              Jessica

Note

Dear Jessica,

Don't be concerned. Everything is on course for tomorrow.

My sincerest apologies for not responding sooner. But I thought I wasn't supposed to leave you any more notes.

Your locker partner,
Ronald

Blue

When I came off the lunch line on Tuesday, I spotted Elizabeth sitting at a table by herself. I headed over there, eager to see how things had gone yesterday. I hadn't had a chance to talk to her all morning.

We need to set up a time to meet this afternoon, I thought. I was already looking forward to that day's lesson. *And I should find out what Rick practiced with her yesterday so I know what we need to do today.*

"Hey," I said, setting my tray down beside hers. "What's up?"

Elizabeth glanced at me, but she didn't smile. "Hi," she said quietly.

I blinked, wondering what was wrong. "Sorry I couldn't make it yesterday. I seriously couldn't get away."

"That's fine," she said blandly.

"Um, so you got the boiled potatoes, huh?" I said lamely, trying to get a read on her weird vibe.

"What?" She looked confused.

I gestured at her tray. "The potatoes."

She stared blankly at the blobby vegetables on her plate for a second. Then she nodded. "Yeah. They looked better than the carrots."

I glanced at the carrots on my own tray. She was right. They did look pretty gross. Pushing the tray aside, I grabbed my OJ and took a sip. "Anyway, how was your lesson yesterday?" I asked. "Was Rick okay?"

"Uh-huh." She still hadn't touched her food. Instead she was gripping the edges of her tray, like she was afraid it was going to fly off if she didn't hold it down. "Actually, I wanted to talk to you about that. Um, I was thinking maybe Rick should keep on training me. You know, from now on."

It took me a second to process that. "What?" I asked, hoping I'd heard her wrong. "What do you mean?"

She shrugged. "It just makes more sense that way," she sort of mumbled. "I mean, Rick happens to have some free time this week. And since you're so busy right now—like with Big Noise and your *Zone* article and stuff—well, anyway, I think Rick'll do a better job coaching me."

My throat tightened, and I couldn't speak at all for a second. I couldn't believe it. She was dissing me? It was all my idea for her to enter the contest, and she was totally blowing me off for Rick? It just didn't compute.

"But it's not supposed to just be my *Zone* article," I croaked out at last. "It's *our* article. The whole point-counterpoint thing. Remember?"

"We can still do that, sort of," Elizabeth replied with a slight shrug. "I mean, you can still write your surfing story. And I'll write mine. They'll just be about our own separate experiences. It will probably be more interesting that way anyhow."

I didn't know what to say. Was she mad at me? It kind of seemed that way. She wasn't really meeting my eye as she talked—she was kind of staring off over my left shoulder, like she found the view out the cafeteria windows totally fascinating. But why?

It couldn't just be because I had to bail yesterday, could it? I wondered.

"Listen, Liz, if you're mad about yesterday, I can explain. . . ."

"No, I'm not mad," she said softly. "I just think it would work out better this way."

"Well, okay, dude, if that's what you want."

Elizabeth nodded. "Would it be all right if I held on to your surfboard for a few days?" she went on. "I promise I'll get it back to you after the competition."

"Sure," I said. "Of course."

"Um, Anna's waving at me," Elizabeth said before I could figure out something else to say. She stood up and grabbed her tray. "I better go see what she wants. See you around." She hurried off toward a table across the room without a backward glance.

I stayed slumped at my own pathetic, lonely loser's table. Part of me sort of wanted to be mad at her—it was pretty lame to just suddenly decide to kick me to the curb. But mostly I was just bummed. I was supposed to be Elizabeth's coach. And somehow, without even realizing it, I'd let her down.

jessica

After school on Tuesday, I decided it was time to hit the beach for a little more sun time. Not that it mattered so much anymore—once the teams were announced tomorrow, I could relax and enjoy the fact that Lacey was going to be far away from me during Olympics week.

I wonder which team Ronald ended up putting her on? I thought idly as I changed into my favorite lavender bikini and tossed some vital necessities, like magazines and lip gloss, into my beach bag. I'd watched him pull up the lists on his computer the other night but hadn't stuck around long enough to watch the whole long process of actually changing the names around. Once he'd heard the pathetic saga of me and Lacey, Ronald hadn't seemed to care that much about having me stick around to "help" anymore. I'd hit the road as soon as possible. *It would be pretty funny if Lacey ended up stuck on a team with a bunch of serious jocks,* I thought. *Or maybe with a whole bunch of dweebs from the math club.*

I giggled out loud at the thought of Lacey Frells surrounded by an army of geeks wielding calculators and pocket protectors. But I decided that little scenario wasn't too likely. Those math dweebs were Ronald's friends—he wasn't going to intentionally inflict Lacey on them.

Whatever, I told myself as I headed downstairs. *I don't care what team she's on as long as it's not mine.*

The closest beach was only a short walk away. When I got there, I saw a bunch of people lying out, taking advantage of the warm afternoon sun. A few people were down by the water too—including my twin and a blond guy with a surfboard.

I grinned and headed over to say hello to the two lovebirds. But when I got a little closer, I suddenly realized that the blond guy wasn't Blue. It was one of his buddies, Rick.

Just then Elizabeth spotted me. She frowned and tugged at the strap of her old purple bathing suit. "What are you doing here?" she asked me.

"I was about to ask you the same question," I replied, raising one eyebrow. "I thought you'd be over at Blue's beach. With Blue."

"I'm just helping your sister learn how to surf," Rick answered for her. I noticed he was staring at Elizabeth with this goofy sort of expression on his face. "She's really good so far. Like, a natural talent. She just needs a little work on her technique."

I grimaced. *Uh-oh. He's got it bad,* I thought. *What, is Liz a surfer-dude magnet or something?*

"I thought Blue was teaching her how to surf," I said loudly. "When did you take over the job?"

Elizabeth shot Rick a slightly nervous smile. "Could you excuse us for a second?" she asked him.

"Sure, dude. No problem." Looking a little confused, Rick wandered off down the beach, glancing at us a few times over his shoulder.

Elizabeth dragged me in the opposite direction until we were out of earshot. Then she whirled on me. "Okay, if it's any of your business, Jessica, I decided Rick should be my teacher from now on," she snapped. "Is that okay with you?"

"No way!" I replied, deciding to ignore her sarcasm. "What happened to Blue? I thought he was your teacher."

Elizabeth shrugged. "Blue's too busy."

"Blue? Busy?" I shook my head. That was a

total contradiction in terms. Blue Spiccoli had to be one of the *least*-busy people I knew. Unless you counted an action-packed schedule of surfing, eating pizza, and playing video games as being busy, that is. "Get real. Since when is he busy?"

"Since he joined Big Noise." Elizabeth frowned. "He even had to cancel on me yesterday. That's when I realized Rick would be a more reliable teacher."

Yikes. It sounded like my little plan had backfired—big time. "Don't be ridiculous, Liz," I said quickly. "You've got it all wrong about yesterday. Blue was all ready to come do your lesson. The other guys practically chained him up and dragged him to those tryouts." Damon had told me all about it.

"Whatever," Elizabeth muttered. "It's not just yesterday. He's got enough to do—rehearsing, all that stuff. He doesn't have time to do this too."

"Are you kidding?" I exclaimed, amazed at how dense she could be. "Those guys only spend, like, five minutes a year actually rehearsing. The rest of the time they're just goofing around. Trust me, Blue has plenty of spare time. And I know he's dying to keep on being your coach."

"It didn't seem like it yesterday," Elizabeth

said, kicking at the sand. "Besides, I like practicing with Rick. He takes it seriously."

I rolled my eyes. She was acting like a total brat. "Look, Elizabeth," I said evenly. "It's obvious you're into Blue, and you're just grumpy because he ditched you yesterday."

"Blue and I are just friends," she said with a frown. "How many times do I have to tell you that?"

"You can tell me as often as you want, but I'm still not going to believe it because it's not true," I replied. "So why don't you just admit the truth? I hope it's not because you don't want me to be right."

Elizabeth didn't answer. She just stared at her feet with this stubborn expression on her face.

I sighed in frustration. Fine. If she was going to be that way, I wasn't going to waste any more time trying to help her. "Whatever," I snapped. "I've got to go. I have better things to do than hang around watching you fool yourself."

Spinning around, I stomped off. I headed down the beach, planning to find a spot far away from my twin and her new teacher. As I reached the top of a dune, I spotted Susie Williams. She was lying on a leopard-print beach towel, listening to some tunes on a Walkman. *What's she doing here?* I wondered. *I never see her on this beach.*

I walked over to her. When she felt my shadow cross her face, she cracked open an eye. "Hey, Jessica," she said, opening her other eye and sitting up. "What's going on? You haven't seen Blue Spiccoli around anywhere, have you?"

"No. He doesn't usually hang out at this beach," I said, a little confused. "He lives right on the water over on the other side of town."

"I know." Susie tossed her long, wavy hair over one shoulder. "I went over to his beach first to look for him. I ran into this guy who knows him, and he said to try over here. He thought Blue might be hanging out with your sister."

"Oh." Now it made sense. And it sounded like Blue's friends weren't fooled by the "just-friends" thing either. "My sister's here, all right," I told Susie. "But not with Blue."

I guess the words came out sounding a little bitter because Susie blinked at me in surprise. "Is something wrong?"

"No, no," I said hastily. "By the way, what happened to you yesterday? I heard nobody showed up for the Big Noise auditions."

Susie nodded. "That's why I was looking for Blue," she explained. "When I talked to you, I totally forgot about this dentist appointment I had, and it didn't end until almost five-thirty."

She pointed to her mouth with a grimace. "By the time I got over to Blue's place, there was no sign of the guys. I was hoping maybe they'd still let me audition."

"Oh! Um, I'm sure they'd be psyched," I said, seeing my plan come back to life right in front of my eyes. So Elizabeth still wouldn't admit she liked Blue as more than a friend? We'd have to see if she changed her tune once tall, good-looking, talented Susie Williams was her non-boyfriend's new band mate. "Come on," I told Susie, deciding my tan could wait. "I'll help you find Blue so you can figure out a good time for your audition."

Elizabeth

I felt my ankles start to wobble as the water swelled under my board. *Focus,* I told myself. *Remember, you* are *the board.*

The words reminded me of Blue. For some reason, that got me wobbling even more. Before I realized it, I had totally wiped out. I went flying off the board just as the wave broke over my head. The force of the wave swept me forward, scraping my hands and knees on the grainy, wet sand and getting salt water up my nose and in my eyes. As I pulled myself to my feet, the board slapped against me, conking me on the kneecap.

"Ouch!" I yelled before I could stop myself. I was tempted to plop down in the shallow water and grab my knee, but I grabbed the board instead. Dragging it after me, I plodded back up onto the dry sand, where Rick was waiting.

"Quite a wipeout," he said when I reached him. "What happened?"

I flopped onto the sand, brushing off my throbbing knee. "I don't know," I admitted with

121

a feeble grin. "I guess it was just the usual problem—gravity."

Instead of laughing, Rick frowned. "You really should try to be more specific," he said. "You've got to, like, study what you did wrong so you can fix it. Otherwise how are you ever going to get it right?"

"I don't know," I muttered, surprised by his attitude.

Blue wouldn't be this uptight, I thought before I could stop myself. *He probably would've said something to make me laugh and feel better about the whole thing.*

"So why don't you tell me what I did wrong?" I snapped, irritated with myself. Why couldn't I stop thinking about Blue? "You're supposed to be the teacher."

Rick bit his lip, looking slightly hurt. I guess my tone was a little harsher than it was meant to be. "Well," he said, "I'm not sure exactly what happened in this case. But you have a tendency to keep your knees a little too straight sometimes. And your feet should probably be a little farther apart. Oh, and if you keep wiggling your head around so much, you'll never really be solidly balanced."

"Gee, am I doing *anything* right?" I retorted, stung by all the criticism. Blue had never ragged on me about any of that stuff. He always said the most important thing was attitude, not exact position. But I didn't bother to tell Rick that. "Maybe I should give up surfing right now and find a different hobby," I muttered. "Like maybe basket weaving."

Rick cleared his throat. "Um, it's getting late," he said. "Besides, I think maybe we both need to chill out for a while. We can start fresh tomorrow. Just think about what I said, okay?"

"Fine." I wasn't about to argue with him. I was starting to think I'd made a huge mistake by firing Blue. Whatever weird personal issues the two of us were having, I definitely missed his laid-back coaching style. Rick was so uptight, he was making me more nervous about what I was doing instead of less.

Maybe I should just go find Blue right now, before it's too late, I thought uncertainly as I gathered up my stuff. Rick was already hurrying off down the beach. *If I ask him nicely, maybe he'll agree to go back to being my coach for the next three days until the competition. Otherwise there's no way I'll be ready.*

I looked over and saw Blue's lucky surfboard lying on the sand. Heading over to get it, I realized I'd been acting like kind of a jerk. Blue had been really nice to me—first helping me through

123

my writer's block, then spending all his free time teaching me to surf—and what had I done to repay him?

Acted like a brat, that's what, I thought ruefully, staring at the well-worn decals on the battered surfboard I was holding. *What's my problem anyway?*

I didn't know the answer to that, and I didn't have time to think about it at the moment. Instead I hurried home to change clothes and drop off my stuff, then took the bus over to Blue's neighborhood. Nobody answered the door at his house, so I headed straight past it to the beach just beyond. It was pretty much his home away from home, so I figured I'd probably find him there.

I was right about that. Blue was at the beach, all right. But he wasn't alone.

Isn't that Susie Williams, from Sweet Valley Middle School? I thought in confusion, recognizing the tall, pretty, auburn-haired girl standing with Blue. *What in the world is she doing with Blue? I didn't even know they knew each other.*

I stood there for a second, wondering if I should go over and join them. It would be better to talk to Blue without an audience, but I didn't want to wait too long. There was no time to waste if I wanted to be ready for the competition on Saturday. And Blue probably wouldn't mind if I broke into his conversation for something this important.

Then again, maybe Blue doesn't want to be interrupted, I thought as Susie tossed her thick, wavy hair over her shoulder and giggled. Blue leaned a little closer and said something. I felt my jaw clench as Susie put a hand on his arm as she laughed hysterically at whatever he was saying. Blue grinned proudly, not seeming to mind one little bit that Susie was falling all over him.

I bit my lip, still wondering what to do. It was stupid, but I couldn't help feeling a little hurt. Not that there was anything wrong with Blue talking and laughing with another girl. It wasn't like he and I were anything more than friends. But still, I found myself backing up, then turning and hurrying away up the beach before he spotted me.

Jessica

I was in an excellent mood when I woke up on Wednesday. Today was the day the school-Olympics teams would be announced, and I was actually looking forward to it now. I couldn't help humming as I poured myself a bowl of cornflakes.

As I sat down at the table and dug in, Elizabeth wandered into the kitchen, yawning and rubbing her eyes. "Good morning," I sang out, shooting her a sunny smile.

Elizabeth mumbled something, then plopped down in her chair. She looked kind of tired, like maybe she hadn't slept that well last night.

I blinked at her. "What's the matter?" I asked.

"Nothing." Elizabeth's voice was subdued and sort of depressed sounding. "I don't want to talk about it."

I shrugged, turning my attention back to my breakfast. I knew I should try to get Elizabeth to tell me what was bothering her, but my mood was just too good to let anything bring me down. *Isn't it great how things just work out for the best sometimes, even when they start out horribly? I thought happily as I crunched my cereal. When Kristin first told me I was on the same team as Lacey, I thought it was the end of any hope I'd have a good time at the school Olympics. But now I can totally look forward to them again. Thanks to Ronald, of all people!*

I almost laughed out loud, thinking about how excited Ronald had been when I'd spilled my story about Lacey. It wasn't something I wanted everyone in the world hearing about, but it had been a small price to pay to guarantee his expert assistance. I actually felt like I owed my locker partner now, big time. Not that I would ever admit that to anyone, of course— least of all Ronald himself.

"What's with you?" Steven asked with a yawn as I skipped past him in the upstairs hall a few minutes later, humming Splendora's newest song. He was still wearing his pajama bottoms, and his brown hair was sticking straight up in two big tufts, making him look like a psychotic bunny. "Since when are you a morning person?" He squinted at me suspiciously. "Wait a minute," he said. "Elizabeth? Are you guys pulling that twin-switch thing again?"

I rolled my eyes. "It's me, Jessica," I said. "I'm

allowed to be in a good mood in the morning if I want."

"Whatever." Steven yawned again and stumbled past me toward the bathroom.

I hurried into my bedroom to get dressed. A few minutes later, as I brushed my hair, I realized I'd left my favorite butterfly clip in Elizabeth's room.

"Knock, knock," I sang out, dancing through our adjoining bathroom and into her bedroom. "Have you seen my—what are you doing?"

Elizabeth was sitting on the edge of her bed, dressed in unbuttoned jeans, her pajama top, and one sock. She was staring blankly into space. When she heard me, she looked up and blinked. "Oh!" she said, jumping up. "I was just—uh—what do you want?"

"Just this." I grabbed my hair clip off her dresser. "Are you okay?"

She bent over to pull on her other sock. "You'd better hurry," she said. "The bus will be here soon."

I shrugged and hurried back to my room to finish getting ready. She was right. It was almost time to head out to the bus stop.

When we got on the school bus, Elizabeth took an empty seat in the middle. I sat down next to her, dropping my backpack on the floor between my feet. "So are you ever going to tell me what's bugging you?" I asked. Okay, so I'm not the most patient person in the world.

"I told you—I don't want to talk about it," Elizabeth replied, shooting me an annoyed glance.

"Talk about what?" I teased.

She frowned. "Just drop it, okay?" she snapped. "I'm not in the mood."

I rolled my eyes. "Don't yell at me just because you've got the *blues*."

Elizabeth didn't respond at all except to frown a little harder. Then she turned her back to me and stared out the window.

I shrugged. Elizabeth was acting really strange, but there wasn't much I could do about it if she wouldn't talk to me. Grabbing my backpack, I pulled out a new sportswear catalog I hadn't had a chance to look at yet. Paging past the boys' clothes at the beginning, I checked out the girls' running stuff, including this killer pair of running shorts—deep blue with a metallic stripe down the side. Maybe I could talk Mom and Dad into buying them for me before the Olympics.

I continued to flip through the catalog for the rest of the ride since Elizabeth was still staring silently out the window. When we arrived at school, Elizabeth and I walked in silence into the building, then I gave my twin a quick good-bye wave and hurried off to my locker.

We don't have homerooms at SVJH the way we did at my old school, so morning announcements happen at the beginning of first period. I grinned when I heard the first crackle of obnoxious static from the PA system. I couldn't wait to hear the team announcements.

I just hope Kristin doesn't get too suspicious, I thought, leaning back in my chair and glancing quickly over at Ronald, who was sitting across the room. He was busy trying to balance his algebra book on a rubber eraser. *But why should she? Computer errors happen all the time. No big deal.*

On the PA system Mr. Todd started off with some boring info about the lunch menu and the next in-service day. Then he cleared his throat. The moment had finally arrived. "And now, students, the announcement you've all been waiting for," he intoned. "I have the official team assignments for the upcoming Sweet Valley Junior High Olympic Challenge. I'll read them to you now."

I looked over at Ronald again. He was sitting up straight and paying attention now. I wasn't sure whether he was interested in hearing the re-

Jessica

sults of his handiwork or if it was just because
his textbook was balanced steadily on the eraser
now. When he saw me looking, he grinned and
held up two fingers in a V-for-victory sign.

Turning away quickly, I grimaced. *Just let the
whole class know we're up to something, why don't
you?* I thought in annoyance.

Still, I couldn't stay too mad at him. I tuned
back in to Mr. Todd. He was reading off the first
team—not mine. I listened for Lacey's name, but
she wasn't on the list.

I guess team number one lucked out, I thought
with a secret smile. *I wonder which team will get
stuck with Lacey?*

I sat up straight when I heard Damon's name
at the top of team number two. "Here we go," I
muttered under my breath.

". . . Mark Williston," Mr. Todd droned. "Jessica
Wakefield. Tony Mason. Sheryl Goldstein. Stacey
Smith. Lacey Frells . . ."

I froze. *Wait a minute,* I thought desperately.
*Wait just a minute here! Lacey isn't on my team. She
can't be! We fixed it!*

I shot a glance at Ronald. This time he didn't
look my way. In fact, he had his head down and
seemed to be staring in complete fascination at
his own fingernails.

Mr. Todd was still listing the members of my

132

team. ". . . Lauren Jervis," he said. "And Ronald Rheece."

Huh? That didn't make any sense at all— Ronald was never on my team in the first place.

Suddenly I had an idea. This was a dream. It had to be. It was still the night before the announcement, and I was just a little anxious, so I was dreaming about what I feared was going to happen. All I had to do was wake myself up.

I gave myself a hard pinch on the leg. "Ow!" I blurted out.

Several people sitting nearby turned to stare at me. I smiled sheepishly and shrugged, then slumped down in my chair with a frown.

This wasn't a nightmare. It was really my life. So now what was I going to do? More specifically, what was I going to do to Ronald?

He was supposed to fix this! I thought furiously. *I mean, I practically watched him do it.* I stopped to think about that for a second. *Well, I didn't actually see him do it, exactly. Come to think of it, all I saw was the original list before I left his house that night. But he was supposed to go ahead and take care of it. . . . He told me everything was on course.* I shook my head grimly. *On course for disaster is more like it.*

I fumed all through first period. As soon as the bell rang, I stomped over to Ronald's desk. "Okay, what's the big idea?" I yelled.

133

"Shhh!" Ronald glanced around the crowded classroom, looking alarmed.

I could see his point. No matter how great my reasons were, I supposed it wouldn't sound too good if people found out what I'd done. What I had *thought* I'd done, that is.

Grabbing Ronald by his skinny arm, I dragged him out into the hall and around the corner to a private spot behind some AV equipment. "All right," I hissed. "Spill it, Rheece. And this better be good."

Ronald cleared his throat, glancing around nervously like a trapped animal. "Er, calm down, Jessica," he said. "Please let me explain."

I crossed my arms over my chest and glared at him. "That's exactly what I'm waiting for," I said coldly. "An explanation. As in, what part of 'get Lacey off my team' didn't you understand?"

"I intended to do as you requested, Jessica, I really did," Ronald said with a shrug. "At least at first. But then, after I heard all your stories about the troubles you've been having with Lacey, I started to think about it some more. I realized it was my civic duty to keep the two of you on that team together."

"What?" I screeched, attracting a few curious glances from passing students. Lowering my voice, I tried again. "What? Why in the world would you think that? I already told you, you were supposed to break us up to protect my teammates and maybe even the whole school from what might happen." Okay, so maybe I was exaggerating just a little, but that's what it felt like.

Ronald was shaking his head. "No, but that's exactly my point," he said earnestly. "See, one of the great psychoanalysts said that a person's ability to be happy is in direct proportion to their being able to deal with things they don't like. So according to that theory, I'm actually helping you by making you face Lacey now. It will be a learning experience. Believe me, you'll thank me in the long run. Besides, life isn't about getting your friends to hack you out of problems, you know."

I was about to give Ronald a huge chunk of my mind when a thought occurred to me. "Hey, wait," I protested. "If all that stuff is true, then why did you hack your way onto my team? You weren't there before."

"Well," Ronald said with a shrug, "I didn't want to leave you stranded."

I sighed, letting my head sink into my hands. "This is a disaster. I can't believe I was actually looking forward to the Olympics up until a few minutes ago," I mumbled into my palms.

"You should still look forward to it," Ronald said cheerfully. "It's all a matter of attitude, Jessica. Mind over matter."

"What?" I looked up with a scowl. What was he babbling about now?

He held up one finger, grinning proudly. "If you don't pay Lacey any *mind*, it won't *matter* to you what she says or does. Mind over matter. Get it?"

I gritted my teeth. The only thing I was getting was an almost overwhelming urge to strangle him. But what good would that do me now? The teams were official.

There was nothing I could do about it.

Elizabeth's Surfing Lessons: Wednesday through Friday

Wednesday

4:00 P.M. Elizabeth and Rick are hard at work.

"Was that any better?" Elizabeth asks breathlessly as she jogs through the shallows.

Rick hesitates. "Sure," he says at last. "It was better. Just a few little things you still need to work on— like the position of your feet and the way you were holding your arms . . ."

Elizabeth sighs and does her best to take in everything he's saying. She has to learn this stuff if she's going to survive that competition on Saturday.

4:23 P.M. Rick tells Elizabeth that she has to focus or she'll never learn anything. Elizabeth frowns and pretends she can't hear him over the crash of the waves.

4:52 P.M. Rick patiently explains that Elizabeth's foot position still isn't right. "Your foot is the foundation of your whole posture on the board," he tells her. "Unless you can get that exactly right, you're never going to be solid out there."

It's funny, Elizabeth thinks as she sighs and heads out to try yet again. *When I first started learning to surf, I actually thought it was going to be fun.*

Thursday

3:36 P.M. As she leaves school on Thursday, Elizabeth is tempted to skip her surfing lesson. She isn't in the mood to deal with Rigid Rick that day. Then she remembers the competition. Squaring her shoulders, she takes a deep breath and heads toward the beach.

4:10 P.M. Elizabeth wipes out for about the fourteenth time that day. "Okay, so what did I do wrong that time?" she asks Rick, wiping salt water out of her eyes.

"You have to remember all the stuff I keep telling you while you're out there," Rick insists for about the fourteenth time that day. "You know, like about your foot position, and your knees, and where your eyes should focus. . . ."

"I can't remember all that," Elizabeth complains. "Can't I just sort of combine them all together? You know—like, just *be* the board?"

Rick rolls his eyes. "Very funny," he says.

5:00 P.M.   Elizabeth still can't get her legs to stay just the way Rick wants them. Feeling frustrated, she offers to go to the hospital and have them surgically attached to the board. In return, Rick suggests they call it a day.

Friday

3:48 P.M.   Elizabeth rushes to the beach after school. There's only one more day of practice before the competition, and she wants to make the most of it.

"Okay, we only have one more day to get me ready for the competition," she tells Rick briskly. "What are we going to work on today?"

Rick shrugs. "The same stuff we worked on yesterday," he says. "You need to get the basics down before you can progress. Your feet, your knees, your balance . . ."

Elizabeth rolls her eyes. She's starting to obsess over her feet, her knees, and various other body parts in her sleep.

3:59 P.M. "Let me guess," Elizabeth says as she drags the board through the shallows, limping slightly from her latest wipe-out. "The problem was my feet."

"Well, yes," Rick says, rubbing his chin thoughtfully. "Also your ankles weren't flexing enough, I think. And your shoulders were too stiff."

Elizabeth is tempted to clonk him over the head with her surfboard. But really, what good would that do?

4:21 P.M. Elizabeth topples off the board—again. "This time I think it was your elbows," Rick says helpfully. "You've got to learn to—"

"That's it!" Elizabeth shouts. "I've had enough."

"Enough what?" Rick asks.

"Enough surfing." Elizabeth picks up Blue's lucky board and stomps up the beach, away from the water. "I'm through," she yells over her shoulder to a surprised Rick.

Blue

I woke up early on Saturday morning, which is kind of unusual for me. At least my brother, Leaf, seemed to think so. "Are you sure you're all right, dude?" he asked me for about the ninety-eighth time as I scarfed down some toast for breakfast.

"I'm fine, okay? Chill," I told him. Gulping some pineapple juice, I checked my watch. The girls' surfing competition was starting in an hour.

What if Elizabeth doesn't want to see me? I wondered as I brushed my teeth. *What if she tells me to take a hike?*

I stared at myself in the mirror, then shook my head. She wasn't like that. If I surprised her by showing up to cheer her on, she'd totally forgive me. I was sure of it.

Well, pretty sure anyway.

Elizabeth had been kind of avoiding me for the past few days. It was pretty obvious she was mad at me, but I still didn't understand why. In any case, I knew I couldn't let things go on this way between us. It would be way too much of a bummer if our friendship got messed up just when things were looking so cool. I couldn't stand it.

I headed down to the beach a little early. For one thing, I couldn't sit still, and Leaf was giving me funny looks. Besides that, I wanted to find Elizabeth before things got rolling.

There were tons of people hanging out, waiting for the competition to start. Most of them were lounging around on the sand, talking and laughing, maybe drinking some coffee. A few of the girls who were entered in the contest were warming up by stretching or jogging in place. A bunch of guys I knew from around the beach had started a pickup game of beach volleyball.

"Yo, Blue!" one of them called to me as I wandered past. "Heads up, dude!"

He tossed the ball to me. I automatically reached up and punted it back, right over the net. "Come on, Blue!" another friend called as he spiked it back over. "Get in here! We need you on our team, man!"

"Sorry, dude," I called back. "Maybe later."

I continued making my way through the crowd. My eyes were peeled for Elizabeth's long, blond hair. But every time I thought I'd spotted her, it turned out to be someone else.

Finally I had to admit it—she wasn't there yet. I checked the time. The competition was starting in fifteen minutes. "She'll be here," I muttered.

I found a spot on a bench up on the boardwalk where I could see anyone heading onto this part of the beach. Then I sat back to wait.

I sat there for about half an hour, until well after the competition got started. People were pouring onto the beach nonstop, but there was no sign of Elizabeth.

Where is she? I wondered, squinting against the glare off the ocean to scan the crowds on the beach. *I couldn't have missed her down there, could I?*

Anything was possible. But somehow I was pretty sure she wasn't down there. In fact, I was starting to think she wasn't planning to come at all.

I slumped down in my seat, wondering what to do. For a second I was tempted to just let it go—forget all about Elizabeth Wakefield, head down to the beach, and hang out with my buds.

But I couldn't do it. I had to fix this thing between us, and it couldn't wait.

There was a pay phone just down the boardwalk. I found a quarter in my pocket and dialed

Elizabeth's number, which I just happened to know by heart.

"Hello?" a male voice answered.

"Uh, h-hi," I stammered. "Is Elizabeth there?"

"I'll see," the voice answered. I couldn't tell if it was her father or her older brother. "Can I tell her who's calling?"

"It's, um, Blue."

"Hold on."

It seemed to take about a million years for Elizabeth to come to the phone. I clutched the receiver tightly, praying that my quarter wouldn't run out before she got there.

Finally I heard the sound of someone picking up on the other end. "Hello?" Elizabeth's voice said.

I cleared my throat. "Elizabeth? Hey, it's Blue."

"I know. Steven told me."

"Oh. Um, can I come over?" I blurted out. "I really want to talk to you."

She hesitated. "Sure," she said finally, though her voice sounded kind of cold. "If you want."

"Great. I'll be there as soon as I can." I hung up the phone and sprinted down the boardwalk toward the bus stop.

Elizabeth

"Sorry it took me so long to get here," Blue said when I answered the door. He shrugged and grinned sheepishly. "I didn't have enough change for the whole bus fare, and the driver was a total troll. He kicked me off twelve blocks from here, and I had to walk the rest of the way."

I glared at him. I wasn't ready to forgive him yet, no matter how cute and breathless he looked. "Really?" I said coolly. "I just figured you suddenly remembered another important band rehearsal or something."

He winced. "Want to take a walk?" he suggested.

I wasn't too sure about that, but I nodded and stepped outside, closing the front door behind me. We walked down the front walk to the sidewalk, then turned and started wandering down the block. For a few minutes neither of us said anything.

But finally Blue cleared his throat and glanced

at me. "Elizabeth," he said. "I'm really sorry. You know, about blowing you off the other day, if that's what you're mad about. That was a totally bogus thing to do. But I really thought you and Rick would do okay."

"Yeah, well, we didn't," I mumbled. I was trying hard to hold on to my annoyance with Blue, but he wasn't making it easy. "Rick was way too uptight about the whole thing."

"Really?" Blue shrugged. "Bummer."

Was that all he was going to say? I frowned. "Yeah," I added pointedly. "The only reason I asked him to keep coaching me was because my original teacher was too busy to help me like he said he would."

"But I wasn't—," Blue began.

"Of course, it's mostly my own fault," I interrupted, kicking angrily at a tuft of grass growing through a crack in the sidewalk. "I never should have set out to compete in something I had no experience with. That was stupid."

"No, it wasn't," Blue protested. "It was brave. And really cool. I mean, Brian did it, right? And I'm sure you would have done fine in the competition. You might even have had fun."

I shrugged. "I guess we'll never know," I muttered.

"Yeah." We walked on in silence for a moment

146

or two. Then Blue glanced over at me again. "So what are you going to write about for *Zone* now?" he asked.

I couldn't hold back a slight smile. "Writer's block," I told him. I'd come up with the idea yesterday when I was panicking about blowing the surfing story by quitting.

Blue grinned. "Excellent!" he exclaimed. "That's such an awesome idea, Elizabeth! I still don't know how you do it."

It was getting harder and harder to stay mad at him. "Thanks," I said. "So how did the auditions for a new bass player go anyway?"

"Not too great." Blue shrugged. "Nobody showed up on Monday afternoon at all. It was totally my fault too."

"What do you mean?"

He grinned sheepishly. "I spelled the band's name wrong on the poster."

"Really?" I blinked, trying to figure out how that would mess things up enough so that nobody would show up for the auditions. "Um . . ."

"Instead of Big Noise, I wrote Big Nose," he explained.

"Oh!" I couldn't stop a giggle from escaping. Big Nose. I giggled again. Before I knew it, Blue and I were both laughing hysterically. "Big Nose!" I exclaimed. "That's hilarious!"

"Yeah! It should have said something like, 'Looking for a band to join? Pick Big Nose!' "

I doubled over with a peal of laughter. "What about 'Big Nose. Don't blow it!' Get it? Don't blow your nose?" That one was pretty corny, but Blue and I started laughing even harder.

Finally we settled down again. I searched my mind, trying to remember why I was mad at Blue. Suddenly I remembered something else.

"Hey," I said, trying to sound casual. "I saw you talking to Susie Williams the other day. She didn't audition for the band?" After seeing the two of them together on Tuesday, I'd remembered that Susie used to play the guitar in this band at our old school.

"Not exactly," Blue replied.

I felt myself go cold. If he hadn't been talking to her about auditioning . . .

"See, it turns out she doesn't really play the bass too well," Blue explained. "So when she heard we really only needed someone on bass, not guitar, she decided it wouldn't work out." He shrugged. "For some reason, I guess Jessica told her she'd be perfect for the band."

"So Jessica's the one that hooked you guys up?" I asked.

"Yeah," Blue replied. "Why?"

"No reason." I shrugged. But I had a sneaking

suspicion that Jessica hadn't been too worried about Susie's musical talents when she'd hooked her up with Blue. I couldn't help remembering our conversation last week—*Let's say Blue started dating some amazing girl tomorrow*, Jessica had said. *Are you telling me you wouldn't be the slightest bit jealous?* I made a mental note to mention this to her later.

Then I shook my head to clear it of those thoughts. Blue was still talking, and I'd totally missed what he was saying.

"What?" I asked. "Sorry, I mean, what did you say?"

He glanced at me in surprise. "I was just saying, it looks like Big Noise is going to stay all guys for the time being. We'll just have to find another way to stand out from the crowd."

I couldn't resist. "I know," I told him. "Why don't you officially change the band name to Big Nose? That would *really* make you stand out."

Blue laughed. And just like that, all my annoyance was gone. It was kind of a relief. I'd spent so much time and energy being mad at him all week—it was exhausting. Now maybe we could go back to being friends again.

We wandered around the neighborhood for a while, talking and laughing. Finally I noticed that it was getting late. "Oops," I said, glancing at my watch. "I have to go. My whole family is driving up the coast to have dinner with some relatives."

"Sounds cool," Blue said, though he looked slightly disappointed. "Um, I'll be at the beach tomorrow if you feel like stopping by. Just to hang," he added hastily. "I won't make you surf if you don't want to, I swear."

"Okay." I giggled. "I'll see you then. And I'll be sure to bring your board. Bye, Blue."

"Later, Elizabeth."

As I waved good-bye and turned toward home, I thought about all the crazy stuff that had happened in the past week. Now that I was feeling better about everything, I realized that maybe I'd overreacted just a tad. Why had I freaked out so much when Blue had to miss one lesson? After all, he'd had a good reason. He'd even arranged for a substitute teacher. It just wasn't like me to be such a brat.

I guess I was worried about the competition, I thought. But I almost immediately shook my head. That wasn't it, and I knew it.

So what was it? Why did I get so upset about it? And even more important, why had I felt so hurt when I saw him talking with Susie Williams?

There was only one answer that made any

sense at all. *Could Jessica be right?* I wondered, feeling my cheeks turning slightly pink. *Is it possible that Blue and I really could be more than friends?*

I smiled, shivering slightly as I headed up my front walk, even though it wasn't the slightest bit cold. I couldn't help turning to get one more look at Blue before I went inside. He had turned around too, and now he gave me this embarrassed, shy little wave—as if he hadn't expected me to see him looking back at me.

Well, I thought as I opened the screen door and walked into the house, *I guess anything is possible.*

Check out the **all-new** ....

(**Sweet Valley Web site—**)

www.sweetvalley.com

New Features

Cool Prizes

The **ONLY** official Web site!

Hot Links

(And much more!)

You hate your **alarm clock.**

You hate your **clothes.**

You're going
to love
Jr. High.